THE PRESIDENT'S ASSASSIN

THE PRESIDENT'S ASSASSIN

A Deep State Thriller

Karen Hagestad Cacy

**Washington insider, David Kelly, learns the hard way:
Losing a wealthy presidential donor can be murder.**

Portal•Publishers

This is a work of fiction. Names, characters, places and incidents are either the product of the author's imagination or are used fictitiously. Any resemblance to actual people, living or dead, or locales is entirely coincidental.

THE PRESIDENT'S ASSASSIN V3
by Karen Hagestad Cacy

ISBN

Print: 979-8-9944200-4-1
eBook: 979-8-9944200-5-8

CRITICAL PRAISE FOR KAREN HAGESTAD CACY

BASED ON THE AWARD-WINNING PLAY, "SAY UNCLE!" AND WARNER BROTHERS DRAFT SCREENPLAY.

This offbeat and intrigue-filled detective story was especially interesting to me for capturing the political scene which is our nation's capital. Karen Cacy, as her Amazon bio indicates, is an old Washington DC hand, with many years of immersion in its political milieu. Other exotic locations from around the world are also richly reflected in her writing. Death by President has such a surprising and dramatic climax, it left me wishing for more. It would spoil the story to explain further. I'll leave it to readers to judge for themselves when they read it – something this fine novel certainly deserves. (I wish four and a half stars were an option.)

Kevin Osborne, Author, *"The Prometheus Connection"*

Why Readers Love Karen Hagestad Cacy:

- **Political Intrigue:** Perfect for fans of *House of Cards* and David Baldacci.

- **Authentic Setting:** An insider's look at **Washington, D.C.** and **Maryland** politics.

- **Complex Characters:** A story where the line between "patriot" and "assassin" is razor-thin.

It is not the critic who counts, not the man who points out how the strong man stumbles, or where the doer of deeds could have done them better. The credit belongs to the man who is actually in the arena, whose face is marred by dust and sweat and blood; who strives valiantly; who errs, and comes short again and again, because there is no effort without error and shortcoming; but who does actually strive to do the deeds; who knows the great enthusiasms, the great devotions; who spends himself in a worthy cause; who at best knows in the end the triumph of high achievement, and who at worst, if he fails, at least fails while daring greatly, so that his place shall never be with those cold and timid souls *who know neither victory nor defeat.*

President Theodore Roosevelt

CHAPTER ONE

Chesapeake Bay, Maryland

Passing over the Continental Divide on his way home, Horace Lechman reviewed his life, the past year, and what had just transpired in Hokkaido.

This time, an innocent man, David Kelly, had come very close to being killed. Clearly, it was time for Horace to resolve the threats that had been leveled at him in the past several months. Probably some crank. But how many cranks make their way all the way to northern Japan to wreak their revenge?

Horace Lechman, 68-year-old founder and president of Lechman Enterprises and presidential donor, had underestimated his adversary. After calling Sybil, his "Lavender Lady" at their home in Middleburg about his plans, he had his driver deliver him straight to his 50-foot motor sailer, "Industry-II," floating at anchor in the Chesapeake Bay, Maryland.

Once there, he was glad to note his peaceful company -- a few egrets on shore and some gulls overhead. An occasional rumble across

1

the water identified a passing cargo ship in the bay's shipping lane on its way into Baltimore, on a northwest heading to the Inner Harbor. He liked it that way. His motor sailor gave him the needed refuge of a beleaguered, busy many who had not yet learned to delegate his affairs to others.

If an ordinary man is threatened, detectives will look in all the normal places – wives, ex-wives, business associates, even so-called friends. But where do they look when the man is a billionaire industrialist, with dealings the world over?

If the man is invested in defense weaponry, will his bank book truly reflect lives that are impacted, even harmed, by tools created in his name? If one of the man's myriad of holding companies suffers losses sufficient to wipe out a couple's retirement portfolio, will the busy man at the top be provided with that level of detail?

And what if there is no reason, save misplaced ideology? As Horace related to his government 'minder,' David Kelly back in Japan, wealthy men often get hung for crimes they never committed. Because a certain portion of the population believes capitalism is inherently evil. Believe that wealthy men are, by definition, up to no good.

A 'fat cat' who hangs with the current President?

Grounds for dismissal.

Mixing mega-wealth with political ambition is always suspect. As a consequence, for the Lechman family, bodyguards, secure travel plans, and eyes on the look-out for mean-eyed assassins or angry investors, were all in a day's work.

They lived careful lives.

They had to.

Lechman, to the casual observer, was riding high. Yet the self-made man tonight considered the possibility of folding his cards and turning away. He feared that day might be upon him. Relying on well-honed instincts, Horace Lechman had come to this place to sort things out.

No "namby-pamby," he was a decisive businessman, a problem solver. A man who meticulously gathered facts, weighed decisions and acted. And while Horace went over in his mind a long list of clients, bankers, and projects, he also focused on one particular individual – his friend, the President.

What if certain key decisions about the man were wrong? What if a mountain of actions were based on lies and fabrications?

Was his trust in the wrong man? A man on the verge of doing something terrible? Something against all humanity?

The ship of state was already in full forward motion.

Could a powerful friend manage to turn things back around?

And if such a powerful friend could manage that, what would become of him?

This was the big leagues. In that rarified air, there are clear winners. But oddly, there are no losers. Only survivors.

Lifting a sailbag onto a shelf below, Horace finished the thought:

"Survivors are the only winners."

He poured himself another Scotch neat as he did his own dishes and brushed down the barbeque grill that hung over the end of the boat. He took comfort in the menial task of cleaning up as he pondered his current predicament.

He had placed his trust in a man not unlike himself. The current President, his friend, also was tall, impressive and self-made. Horace had met enough trust fund boys along the way to appreciate a scrapper like himself. President Matthew Walker was from the South. And he was the smartest man Horace had ever met. Walker could hold forth on any book, sports trivia, or even the latest scientific discoveries.

He, like Horace, drew in knowledge as though it were oxygen needed for life. . . . Knowing is always best, both men believed.

Lechman and Walker – different generations – but also, two sides of the same coin. There was a deep and unspoken understanding between the two. Not only could they speak for hours, but they could also sit together without uttering a word, so strong was their friendship. Lechman had a son, and he had two daughters. But none of his children had captured his heart as Matt Walker had.

"Charmed."

The sound of his own voice startled him. But that was exactly it. He had been charmed by Matt Walker. Even when Walker was in the middle of his well-known political two-step, Lechman would give him a pass, understanding the need for expediency in certain situations. But the reason for Lechman's support went far deeper. Because Matt Walker was Horace Lechman. And Horace Lechman was Matt Walker.

Until now.

Lechman had come to "Industry-II," his refuge, his floating home anchored in a tight cove on the Chesapeake Bay, to think. And he was still no closer to answers than he had been the day before in Hokkaido.

At his direction, the fine boat was stocked with several CD's, mostly Mozart, his favorite music, a bottle of fine, aged scotch whiskey, steaks from his butcher Francois at Dean and Deluca Foods by his Georgetown town home, and a briefcase holding his attorney's most recent revision to his Last Will and Testament.

"Matthew Walker, you disappointing son of a bitch." Again, Horace's words echoed oddly in the silence of the plush cabin.

His cell phone rang. It was Sybil.

"Yep. Darlin'. Aw, 'course I'm alright."

Lechman's words were slurred a little from the late hour – midnight – and the effects of a few too many post-prandial drinks.

"How was your evening? . . . That's good, that's good. . . . D'ya run into Matthew? . . . A no-show, eh? . . . Not surprised. . . . All he's been up to lately. . . . Ah, nothing . . . Nothing, my love . . . Not for your pretty little head."

6

As they spoke, Horace stroked a perfumed, hand-written note opened on his counter.

"Now you go on and get yourself some sleep, and I'm going to do the same. Yes, yes, I'll weigh anchor early. Ralph'll be here to finish up. What say the two of us get ourselves off to Montego for a month or so. Sound good? Alright, favorite lady. My turtle dove."

Horace felt the boat tip as the winds picked up outside the cabin window. He poured one more nightcap and ascended the beautiful teak steps to the cockpit. Storm coming up. Nothing to Horace, who had seven Atlantic crossings under his belt, three of which were onboard "Industry-II," a solid blue-water boat if ever there was one. She drew too many feet of water to navigate the Chesapeake Bay's notoriously shallow shores. However, the boat came equipped with a state-of-the-art keel modifier, which Horace had activated, making the big boat's draft shallow enough for overnight camping in this secluded cove off Gibson Island.

In addition, he had three anchors how holding her in the triangulation he had practiced over the years. All was in order. He secured a couple of loose lines that were flapping. Other than that, "Industry-II" was as safe a spot as anyone could be on earth, storm or no storm.

Meanwhile, as the moon shifted behind storm clouds, a large black Jimmy with tinted windows eased its way through the tollgates of the Chesapeake Bay Bridge. Once past the guards' station, the driver pulled to the side of the road as the two men inside closely studied a map.

"Here's Tilgman Island," said the passenger, a man with red hair and stubby fingers whose nails were chewed beyond their cuticles to red, raw flesh.

"Yeh, that's the spot alright," answered the driver, a tall blond man with overlong sideburns and aviator's reflective sunglasses perched on his head, despite the lateness of the hour. In the increasing winds and rain, the driver quickly located the exit, and the hulk of a car made its way down to the water. To a tight and secluded cove. . . . To Horace Lechman's refuge . . . To the "Industry-II."

There was the uncharacteristic smell of a newborn baby as the two men applied talcum powder to their stripped-down chests. The powder would ease the way as the men pulled tight black rubber wet suits over their bodies.

Horace was finishing his evening of thinking with Mozart's Piano Concerto No. 15 in B flat major, one of his favorites. His unsteady gaze had fallen upon a photograph on the cabin's teak wall. It showed his wedding day, when he had married wife number four, Sybil. But he was not thinking about his marriage to a woman many disliked, but who had invested her considerable feminine wiles a hundred percent onto him. The lavender suits, and strong scent of jasmine, the attitude, attributes maddening to most, hid a warmth, caring and all-around intelligence and practicality he needed at this stage of his life.

"Turtle dove."

No more blonds. "My God, I have had my share . . ."

No more women young enough to be one of his daughters. Now, in Horace's end years, he had finally chosen well. He had a true partner. Someone as sharp as a tack, and as protective toward him as a female pit bull. He liked that in a woman.

Horace's attentions slurrily turned to the man standing between them in the photograph, Matthew Walker. The prodigal son. Sporting the $150,000 capped teeth Horace had bought for him during an earlier Senatorial campaign. Raising his glass to those teeth, Horace could feel his own teeth revealing themselves in a snarl.

"Here's to you, Matty boy. . . . You sneaky, weak son of a bitch! You won't be President for long. Watch your back, you scum-sucking sorry piece of . . . a . . . ah . . ."

Horace's words were interrupted by the tug of a garrote being tightly drawn around his neck. As he staggered to turn free, he received a hard fist jammed to his right kidney. But even though this attack was unexpected, and Horace was under the influence of too many drams of his fine scotch whiskey, there were some things in his favor. His size, for instance. It takes more than a garrote and one fist to the gut to fell a man of Horace's size and physical stamina, the two black-suited frogmen soon learned.

The intelligence and size of the man quickly came into play as adrenalin put the magnate into full survival gear. He grabbed a gold paperweight – one coincidentally given to him by the "Southern Prince," Walker –slamming it full force into the first man's temple. The unexpected blow sent the man reeling backward, spurting blood from his head wound onto the beige duck slip-covered berth.

Now the second man, jumped onto the map table, tackled Horace, and grabbed the open scotch bottle, smashing it against the bulkhead. He placed the jagged edge close to Horace's throat as the other man pressed his knees into Horace's chest.

"Mr. Lechman, we have an important message from a friend of yours."

As Horace twisted half-way upright again, the second man whipped out a Sony Walkman and activated a tape.

"Horace, I'm sorry it had to come to this. I am afraid that you are no longer understanding of the seriousness of what it is we are trying to accomplish. You were always like a father to me. But now, unfortunately, it's survival time. Turns out I'll be needing that money from your estate sooner than expected. This next campaign, I am told, is going to be brutal. Everyone and their uncle's lining up to take us on. Don't worry. I'll see that your family is well taken care of. And I know how you loved the symphony. I'll see that a wing of the new hall is named after you. Least I could do. See you on the other side, buddy."

As these words hit Horace's ears, an odd reaction set in. His muscles relaxed underneath the two men. It was as if everything he had dared not believe was confirmed in the taped message. Not some crank, after all. The son. He had been betrayed by the 'son.' The air left his lungs even before the smooth, sharp glass shard glided across his jugular vein. Before the quarts of warm, thick blood flowed onto the polished teak deck.

And as Horace's eyes lost their intelligence, and death cloaked them into a sightless gaze, the two men carefully gathered up his loose papers along with his briefcase and placed them into a watertight pouch. Then set the fire. And slipped overboard. And swam to shore. And cleaned themselves up. Changed clothes, lit cigarettes, as though they had just had sex in a French film. And headed back over the bridge.

As the driver negotiated the Jimmy through the storm, he looked at his watch. Twelve-forty-five. They had arrived at Twelve-thirty. Sometimes the time between life and death can be fifteen minutes. Just fifteen minutes. His companion busied himself with the pouch. Both men kept souvenirs from their work.

The passenger, Frank, to his friends, put on a Spanish accent as he handed the driver his.

"Here you go, compadre. This will provide you with -- how you say in your language, 'protection,' from your very fine employer."

The assassins knew the one who ordered this job would not hesitate to offer up the same medicine for them if the need arose. It's never good to know too much. One needed extra insurance to conduct such a life. Accordingly, tonight each man took out his own 'Lechman life insurance policy.'

As the saying goes, 'A little something for a rainy day.'

The driver finally spoke: "Handy little bay, the Chesapeake."

'Frank,' to his friends, responded, "We've gotta get real jobs one of these days."

The two men laughed as the driver responded.

"Beats Guatemala, cupcake. Beats Guatemala."

CHAPTER TWO

Three days earlier, Sea Tac Airport

If looks could kill, David Kelly would be dead.

Normally, Cabinet Secretary Jeffrey Layton, was an approachable man of impeccable manners, old world charm, and formidable intellect. Not tonight. Tonight, seated in SeaTac's V.I.P. departure lounge, "massah" was in no mood. Kelly had innocently misread his boss by asking a question about their trip. It was a simple question, he thought.

"Why Japan?"

"What d'ya mean, why Japan?"

"With all the needy countries, why are we beginning our resource development program in one of the world's richest? And what does Horace Lechman, a presidential donor, have to do with anything?"

"Oh."

By Layton's non-answer, he should have known better than to continue. But continue he did.

"Japan, I mean."

The Secretary huffed, slapped his newspaper down on the table and barked to no one in particular, "Can we get a cup of coffee in here?" His sharp tone caused a V.I.P. lounge attendant to hop to, presenting them both with coffees and pastries set out on a silver tray.

Thereafter, the two men continued their trip mostly in silence. Normally, David's mentor was even-tempered. Tonight, however, something was amiss -- trouble at home -- he wondered? In any event, the hour was late, the flight long, and David Kelly felt relieved not to have to interact with anyone, especially a cranky boss.

Instead, he spent the long flight across the Pacific reviewing the past eight hours spent in Seattle. The memory of his day, not unlike memories of his life with his former wife, Julie, was already a blur. The mind can play tricks when thoughts are too raw, too close to the surface.

David felt uncomfortable taking the Secretary's showy car to his old neighborhood. He knew Julie would make some smart remark about it. She would view the car as an imposition – there he goes again, trying to be important, showing off.

David Kelly, Assistant Secretary for Legislative Affairs, Department of Resource Development, was a bureaucrat the news media mostly avoided. Honest. Hard working. Idealistic. At least he had been once, years earlier. And now? Still honest. Still hard working.

But idealistic? No longer. Years of accommodation to Capital Hill whims and fancies had taken their toll. David Kelly was fed up with all of it. The outsized egos, seeing sound policies watered down to next to nothing, watching the quick-fix artists blow through town for the "government service" notch on their holsters.

With a third glass of red wine, he could admit to himself Julie had been right to pull the plug on Washington. Of the two of them, she was the one with the common sense. She did not suffer fools or self-important people lightly. David laughed to himself. Once Julie eliminated 'official Washington,' it was a short step to eliminating him as well.

Well, fuck her and her narrow life. Fuck the Seattle Sail Club. Fuck everyone whose life centers around building a new fireplace in the outside patio.

Still, as a perfectly done steak with béarnaise sauce was placed before him on a tray, David pictured in his mind Julie's girlish red curls poking from beneath her work bandanna, and the trim fit of blue jeans she had worn since college days. Maybe she missed him as much as he missed her. Missed their real life together.

Fucking dreamer. Get real.

Still, as he left their former home that was in need of paint, with the broken steps and falling down rose trellis, the pretty girl he always thought was out of his league, managed one final put down. What was it she said? Oh, yeah.

"Give the Secretary my best. You always have."

But there were even worse memories of his day in Seattle. There was Scooter, the family dog, growling at him as he approached. There was his ten-year old, Josh, seated outside the home, hugging Scooter as though his life depended on it. There was Kenny, his twelve-year old out sailing with Ernie Fields. He had so much to make up to his boys. Clearly, his life in Washington, DC was no good for their young lives in Seattle. The boys needed a father. And Kelly needed his boys.

With these troubling thoughts, David Kelly took little notice of the oceanic turbulence as the big jet passed south of the Hawaiian Islands. His eyes closed over the alcohol, as his subconscious mind worked to sort things out, to make sense of his life.

Meeting a fat cat presidential donor. Announcing the President's plan to fund a new Ainu Indian resort in Hokkaido; be nice; be the government lap dog, happy boy faces, with the wind to their backs.

Yet, if one were to analyze it, in his restless dream existed the seeds of a new life. Seamless separation from his job . . . Purchase of a fancy liveaboard at the Bellevue Marina . . . a slender redhead with dancing green eyes onboard to share . . . David heard himself call out to his sons that their eggs were ready. . . saw them proudly man the tiller as they sailed their tiny Sunfish past David's line of sight, as he sipped his second cup of coffee seated on his teak after- deck.

But then, REM's took him backwards once again. Backwards seemed to be David's only direction lately. The damned gear shift was jammed. The gear shift of his damned life.

Again, he was seated across the kitchen table from Julie. Did he see a flicker of regret in her eyes? Probably not. She was telling him, "Here's a form I need you to sign. Gives Kenny permission to race in

19

the Sound. He's been quite the little crew member for Ernie Fields. You remember Ernie, don't you? Anyway, Ernie's been thinking about racing the TransPac, and Kenny has been filling in whenever one of Ernie's real crew can't make it. It's a big, fast safe boat. I think you've seen it. And, as you know they are all crack racers. Kenny is having a ball doing it and . . ."

She talked on. Each time she came to the name 'Ernie Fields,' he felt like he was being kicked in the stomach. The woman he had loved all these years? Gone. The son he had first taken sailing? On loan to another man. The house he had purchased to renovate? Falling down. Yeh, that about summed things up.

"Ernie Fields, my ass," he muttered.

Julie looked up to catch a look at his face, seeming not to hear. "What?"

"I said, Ernie Fields, my ass. That's what I said. Julie, for Christ's sake!"

She simply stared at him as she would an interesting piece of driftwood. He knew he had no further rope left on that subject. He turned to his job, another no-win subject with her.

Looking at her passive face, he told her only the briefest of information about the trip to Japan. Told her about the Far East development consortium they had formed. About his promotion by Secretary Jeffrey Layton for work ongoing on the President's landmark bill to help save the world's wilderness areas.

As usual, she was unimpressed. "Good for you."

The loud thump of landing gear awakened David.

Then, the big jet landed.

"Ernie Fields, my ass," David muttered as the plane's wheels finally touched pavement.

CHAPTER THREE

Hokkaido, Japan

"Please to have some tea, sir?"

The young woman was careful in her speech, speaking English with a heavy Japanese accent, not surprising here in this remote health spa on Japan's wintry northern island just south of the long-disputed Sakhalin Islands, location of Russia's space and defense testing.

"Ee-yeh, arrigato gozaimasu," said David Kelly, practicing his limited knowledge of Japanese. He had been on this island thirty years earlier as an enlisted man repairing complex U.S. government listening devices, a fact he failed to mention to the Secretary. His four-year military assignment gave Uncle Sam two extra years in exchange for not drafting him and shipping him off to Vietnam. Mainly, he remembered how damned cold it was here, catching the wintry winds off Siberia.

David tried to accompany his refusal with a warm smile but given the hour and state of his jet-lag, he was sure his face betrayed a rude disinterest in the woman and her kind offer.

23

"Please. Very good. We add sake and certain other of ingredients. You will enjoy. Please." The woman was not going away. David finally took the time to notice her. She was not Japanese, but Ainu Indian. This ancient Indian tribe had long inhabited Hokkaido, particularly here around the hot springs area of Noboribetsu on the southern coast of the island.

The woman was stunning. High cheekbones, round limpid brown eyes, nearly cartoonish they were so large. Long, silky blue-black hair twirled around her waist. As she leaned into the sofa, he detected a most pleasant flowery scent. Suddenly, his senses awakened. And as he took his first long sip of the warm, redolent alcoholic tea, he felt instantly cheered and revived. The trip, so long and tiring, seemed to be looking up. He remembered now. He was to wait with the bags here in the lobby while Layton checked them in.

David Kelly. Age 50, with close-cropped wavy black hair revealing grey at the temples, tortoise shell eyeglasses perched precariously atop his head, uncurled his trim, medium frame from the too-small Japanese couch.

Profession: Deputy Assistant Secretary for Legislative Affairs to Secretary Jeffrey Layton head of the U.S. Department of Resource Development.

Personal Life: You've got to be kidding. Divorced. Two children, Josh and Kenny, aged ten and twelve.

Current Mission: Attendant to one over-wrought cabinet secretary and his billionaire presidential buddy.

Real Mission: Frankly, murky. Not making a helluva a lot of sense anymore.

Oh . . . that David Kelly.

Slowly, as the tea and liquor mixture warmed him, the room came into focus. He was not seated on the aft deck in Friday Harbor. Far from it. Rather, he was in snowy Hokkaido. To hold industrialist, Horace Lechman's, hand as he announced the development of an Indian resort. And to experience first-hand the wonders of President Walker's global wilderness legislation, yet to be passed by the U.S. Congress.

And that, catching himself up, was where he came in. David Kelly, reporting for duty, sir. One landmark bill, coming right up!

Back in Washington, as closely as he could recall, prior to this odd trip, he had been minding his own business crafting environmental and land use laws. David had a reputation for his ability to merge policy, politics and procedure into the right combinations to achieve

25

legislative triumphs. It was exactly that reputation, as well as his long-held political ties in Washington State, which had landed him his current job in the Administration.

As the tea-sake mixture travelled south warming his throat, then chest cavity, the Ainu woman carefully refilled his ceramic cup. David began to unwind, taking a long look around at his surroundings. Two hours ago, they landed at Sapporo International Airport from Seattle. They were met at customs by Lechman's personal chauffeur. They were whisked to an elegant black Daihatsu limousine equipped with wet bar, the latest stateside papers, reading light and pristine white linens on the head-rests.

The driver, a muscular fellow, was dressed in full black livery, black chauffeur's cap, and white cotton gloves. On the radio, during their trip 40 kilometers south to the Noboribetsu Hot Springs Resort, played a popular Japanese hit parade of tunes.

As the car made its way south through the snowy northern Japanese countryside, Layton offered David a copy of Lechman's profile, provided by the White House.

"Of course, I know the man personally, due to my long friendship with his wife, Sybil. Helluva man, I can tell you. But don't take my word for it. Have a look."

With those words Layton handed him the confidential "Eyes Only" report.

According to the report, Lechman was currently married to wife number four, Sybil. His first three wives had been younger and blonder, the mothers respectively of his three children, now grown. One wife was an oft-incarcerated alcoholic.

David was amazed at the level of personal trivia in the report. Did they have such detail on everyone, he wondered, or just the odd billionaire? He read on, fascinated.

Another wife had only recently given up filing numerous lawsuits, attempts to procure more of Horace's fortune. The third ex-wife had married her divorce lawyer. Sybil, number four, had opened her arms and their homes to Horace's eighteen-year-old, a troubled boy who desperately needed mothering. The Lechman frequented an impressive real estate portfolio of homes in Washington, Virginia, Montego Bay and London.

Once David came to the end of the written profile, he recalled the rest of the story, as recounted by a fawning national media:

---Horace Lechman had no idea what his real name was, having been left in a basket on the steps of the Mission for Hadassah Charities in St. Louis as a six-day old infant.

---His near-genius I.Q., inborn drive to succeed and considerable physical advantages had propelled him far beyond the mid-American St. Louis.

---He now headed a vast multi-national conglomerate engaged in banking, energy concerns and defense industries.

--- The current president owed his office in no small measure to the Lechman tab.

It occurred to David that he probably knew more about Horace Lechman than he did about some members of his own family.

"What a country!" he thought.

In Washington, the Secretary had introduced him to Lechman, explaining to them both the President's wish that Horace be accompanied on the Japan mission. The mogul had been cordial, if a little distant at the news. Lechman was to precede them onboard his private jet, and they were to arrive later via First Class on commercial carrier. The three were to meet up at the resort.

A strangely nervous Jeffrey Layton attempted to explain David's role. From his halting explanation, couched in lofty verbiage about the Wilderness Policy, David came away with the conclusion that he was being included mainly to serve as Lechman's lap dog. He was to be the government poodle brought along to fetch, carry and do tricks. He was to be deferential, even subservient. At all times, he was to remember that Lechman was the President's good and true personal friend.

In his forties, David would have jumped at the chance to travel to Japan on the government's tab, whatever the pretext. Now? He preferred staying behind at the office. But the Commander in Chief had spoken. As civil servant, it was David's job but to comply.

Now seated in the rustic lobby of the up-scale Japanese resort, he appeared to be the only American. The chairs, set among Japanese tansu chests atop priceless Taiwanese Oriental rugs, were oddly covered in plaid fabrics reminiscent of a Montana hunting lodge. Globalism, David concluded, could go too far. At least they had refrained from erecting dead animal heads over the roaring fireplace.

Following the two-hour car trip capping off the long plane trip, they were on time and ready to meet up with their charge. Despite the warming refreshment, David's fatigue was starting to take its toll once again. As his head began to nod, he noticed the polished shoes of the concierge parked in front of him. Looking up, a small silver tray was presented. On it was a card bearing a United States flag – he recognized it as Layton's personal card.

The message was written in an old-fashioned, flowery ink pen script.

"David. Sorry that I have been detained. Must make urgent calls. Please go ahead and check yourself in. Plan on dinner around seven. J.L."

David gave a nod to the bell hop hovering nearby with the luggage. The young Ainu woman carried his drink as the three of them made their way to his room in the rustic ryokan. Craftsman wood trim detailed his small, but luxurious suite. Inside, the bell boy accepted his tip and left.

The woman gently removed his suit jacket and began unpacking and hanging his clothes in the closet. She then showed him how to open the window should he desire fresh air. In this climate? Sub-zero ice and snow? Not bloody likely! Then she directed him to a low platform, rolling out feathery bedding atop a futon. Finally, she opened the liquor cabinet and handed him a small map to the spa and restaurant.

"Girl will come for bath, one hour."

With those words, she left the room, trailing her perfume and memory of black tresses along with her.

As David lay back on the soft pillows, all his questions seemed to melt away. Gently, he drifted off. He was skiing down a powdery mountain. Then he was touching a woman's silky black hair. As he flashed from scene to scene in a fitful dream, the hour passed. Finally, he heard a voice, and again, took note of a woman's scent, but a different one this time.

Another woman, also Ainu and beautiful, was in the room, removing a large robe from its hanger. As he wakened she had crossed to the futon and began removing first his socks, and then his trousers. David was too sleepy to resist. Oddly enough, her undressing of him was businesslike, as one would undress a child for his bath. Once he was fully naked beneath the large robe, the woman led him down the hall to the baths.

Outside, the icy air mixed with the hot springs steam rising from the pools. His escort handed him off to another woman who swiftly removed his robe, dunked him in a private pool and proceeded to scrub him all over with brushes and soft sponges. Once finished, he was led to a "rinsing" pool. Finally, he was deposited in a third steamy pool. A teak tray floated near him providing more of the hot tea concoction, as well as bottled water.

David could barely see where he was, so thick was the steam rising up in the outdoor pool. A voice very near him gave him a start.

"Mr. Lechman. How do you do. Your trip, I trust, was comfortable?"

David began to correct the man, but he waved his arm at him and continued.

"Ah, just have another sip of that aged whiskey, my friend. Then, a fine dinner. Your country's helpfulness in the face of Japan's land shortages is highly appreciated."

What the devil? David thought.

"The woman has already left a small remembrance for Matthew in the Secretary's room. We look forward to a long and worthwhile partnership. Please tell Matthew how much we are honored by his friendship. And enjoy your stay. Your plane has been cleared for takeoff anytime tomorrow at your leisure. No, no need to get up. Enjoy. Steam. Cleanse the soul here in Hokkaido's pristine wilderness. 'Pristine.' Is a good word, no? Shows you how excellent our English training is nowadays. Actually, I may have learned that word at Yale. You are a Yale man, yes? Enjoy, sir. Enjoy."

Before David could speak the man had disappeared back into the steam. He went back over what the man had said in his mind, the better to tell Layton of the odd conversation over dinner. Just then, two loud reports sounded. The first tore up the water immediately in front of him. The second whizzed just past his left ear. Faster than he thought he could move, David scrambled out of the pool. His leaden arms gained new strength as the adrenaline of terror kicked in, full bore. He grabbed a towel and searched for a door.

He seemed to be the only one in the outdoor room, except for the gunman. Too close for comfort once again, he heard the sound of breaking glass followed by another gun shot. He had to get the fuck out of here. What was going on anyway?

Was someone trying to kill Horace Lechman? Or was this some sort of local sport – 'shoot the tourist.' For some reason, as his hands desperately felt along the wooden wall for the door, his brain was doing an out-of-body comedy routine.

"I know Japanese-American relations aren't perfect, but this is ridiculous."

He recalled that Japan worked to keep a million of its citizens off the islands on vacation at any one time, due to over-population. Were they also killing off visitors, as part of that policy? David knew he had to get a grip. Because being shot at was no laughing matter. Still, as his feet were slipping and sliding along the wet tile floor of the spa, he wondered at the sheer ridiculousness of his situation.

Stubbing his toe, he fairly flew through an open door. Relief. He landed in a carpeted hallway near the lobby. Nice, safe hallway. God bless hallways, he thought. Clutching a towel around his bare waist, and dripping water, David quickly made his way to the lobby. Instinct told him a public place with people would be safe.

There, a bizarre site greeted several newly-arrived tourists standing inside the entryway – a freaked out American man, skin puffy and red as a lobster from the spa, dripping water over the costly rugs, clutching a too-small white bath towel around his middle. Near- naked men with crazed eyes in the lobby had not been mentioned in the ryokan's sales brochure.

Outwardly, the courtly concierge showed no reaction. But, David could tell by a certain cast in the man's eyes, he was intending on removing him from his lobby as soon as decorum would allow.

"Someone's shooting at me in the pool!" David fairly screamed.

Reacting to him as though he were a mental patient off his meds, the concierge smoothly replied, "Sir, I can assure you, nothing like that could have happened here. What shooting? We would have heard any disturbance."

"Please to allow Hiroko to accompany you back to your room. I am sure it was all a misunderstanding. Perhaps the sake and hot bath created confusion. I assure you sir, all is fine . . . once you get some rest . . ." And with that, Hiroko, the Ainu woman with the flowery perfume took his arm and led him patiently back down the residential hallway, unlocking his room, making reassuring clucking sounds all the while.

"Dinner is at seven, Kelly-San."

He was alone again.

What the fuck?

David quickly locked the ryokan room door from the inside, then checked the window locks. All seemed in order. With shaking hands, he poured himself a drink. He glanced at his watch. Fifteen minutes before he was due to meet Layton and Lechman for dinner. And, speaking of Layton, where was he? Maybe he should try to call his room. Glancing at the phone with Japanese Kanji script, David pondered how to use the contraption.

"Ponder quickly, asshole, because people shooting at you definitely requires your full attention," David lectured himself.

Then he remembered his good friend Max Berfield. Former Special Forces, now a war correspondent based in Washington. He needed to talk to someone who would take him seriously. Preferably before dinner. After dinner, there might be more target practice.

The front desk connected him practically immediately.

"Max. Max, goddamn it, I am so glad you're at home."

"David? That you? Why the hell wouldn't I be? It's three-fucking a.m. here. Where the hell are you?"

"Long story. Northern Japan. Listen, I need to ask you about something. And promise you will hear me out before you say anything. Max? You there?"

"Fire away, buddy."

With that, David told him the story. As much of the story as he knew. Finishing,

"So, what do you think? Am I nuts? What should I do here?"

Max's considerable combat experience kicked in, as he responded in a serious tone.

"Well, 'A,' whoever shot at you in the pool thought you were this guy Lechman, sounds like. And 'Two,' I'd stay the hell away from that guy for the rest of the trip. Matter of fact, I'd think strongly about curtailing further spa activities and hopping the next bird outta there. Pronto."

"Can't. I'm due to meet Layton and Lechman for dinner in a few minutes, and then of course, we are finishing up our business before we leave tomorrow."

"Business? What kinda business?"

"Max. You've been in government work long enough to know . . ."

"Yep. Sorry. But listen, if something's beyond your job description, it's time to speak up my friend."

"Well getting shot at is definitely above my pay grade! Hey, listen. I'd better get off now. Any last thoughts on what I do tonight to stay alive?"

"You sleeping on a futon?"

"Yes."

Max advised, "Move it." Keep the lights off. Take heavy furniture, stack it up at the door. And, buddy, one last word of advice . . ."

"What's that?"

"Sleep with your fucking eyes open."

CHAPTER FOUR

"I'm sorry. This table is too close to the others. We can't sit here . . ."

Who said that? What had he just done? David, joining the Secretary for dinner, heard his own out-of-body voice reject an elegant table set for them near the restaurant's fireplace. Lit candles, fresh flowers and white linens provided a perfect setting for their celebratory V.I.P. dinner party.

Horace Lechman was nowhere in sight. The other diners, David noted, were elegantly attired and not one of them resembled his idea of a gunmen. He began to feel like an idiot. He was too jumpy. There was no attempted murder. Wasn't that what the concierge had said? Perhaps that sake he'd been drinking all afternoon was really some kind of Far Eastern absinthe that destroys the mind and fosters paranoid delusions.

Yes, that was what it was. He was being a real jerk, unfit for polite company. And yet, in the real world . . . at least in David Kelly's version of the real world . . . one doesn't fly to some God-forsaken Indian spa in Japan to have dinner with a billionaire. He was a legislative analyst, for God's sake! Nothing more, nothing less.

Perhaps entry into this rarified air had been too much for him. He had a case of the bends. That was it. The bends.

Secretary Jeffrey Layton was startled by his aide's peculiar request. He already had noted Kelly's appearance, disheveled, not the way a man presents himself at a business dinner in an elegant resort with a cabinet member and one of the President's most generous donors.

With a sigh, Layton picked up his drink glass and napkin he had carried in from the lobby with him. "Fine. You pick the table. By all means." Layton decided to humor David, at least temporarily. But soon, this sort of behavior would have to stop.

David selected a table in the very back of the room near the kitchen, a table in no man's land that no one, much less such stellar guests, would accept. The startled wait-staff began to comply, but it was too much even for them. With many bows and tones of wounded deference, they urged the men to reconsider. The first spot was, after all, more in keeping with their status. Layton, relieved, shrugged his shoulders at David, and the two finally took their former seats.

As they were seated before the fireplace, Layton ordered a bottle of wine.

"Our guest seems to be a bit late this evening."

40

David took a sip of the wine. Was now a good time? No, Lechman might show. This was one conversation David knew ought to be confidential. Instead, he kept to business at hand.

"So, the ceremony takes place tomorrow morning?"

Layton explained. "The Mayor of Sapporo will be here. A few Ainu representatives. Some Japanese businessmen. Lechman will sign the contract, a few photos will be taken, and back we go again."

"Seems like a long ways to come only for that . . ."

"Yes, well . . . I wonder what is keeping our guest."

Layton signaled the waiter for a house phone. He dialed Lechman's room. There was no answer.

Finally, David waded in.

"Maybe someone killed him."

"David! That is so very not amusing."

"No, really. Some guy started talking to me in the spa this afternoon – addressed me as Lechman. He said he left some money for you for Walker. D'you get it?"

Layton nodded.

"He left. And then someone started shooting at me. Or Lechman. Whoever. I ran like hell. That was my afternoon. Like I said, maybe someone killed Horace Lechman. Later, I mean. After they missed me."

Jeffrey Layton just sat there, staring at David. As David watched his face, he read a range of emotions. First was distraction, at his ridiculous story. Then anger. Then – David was certain of it -- fear.

The Secretary dropped his voice.

"Alright then. Strange story. I shall search the hotel for our guest. You contact Lechman's driver. Tell him we will be needing to take off tomorrow right after the meeting. No use hanging around here. Got me?"

Layton didn't need to paint David any pictures. He knew quite well that when one is keeping company with someone who's a target, one would do well to keep one's distance. It was a directive David had every intention of following.

The wait staff was bringing plates of appetizers, fussing around them, filling their drink glasses, sweeping breadcrumbs away. Layton knocked over his water glass. When a man came to clean it up, he barked at him, "Please leave us. We are trying to have a conversation!"

"Now then. Now then. You finish up here. And I'll see you in the a.m."

With that, he was gone. David remained seated, with a table full of food, and a mind full of thoughts. He finished up a bowl of rice and all of the remaining sake. Was he becoming an alcoholic, he wondered? No, just a stressed-out sack of nerves. What a night. What had his friend said? To sleep with his fucking eyes open? No problem. He knew he would not relax again until he was all the way back home. With his tropical fish and one of Kenny's frayed teddy bears in the bed guarding his sleep.

Back in his room, his futon had been laid out. A large down comforter looked inviting. David began getting undressed when he heard a sound. It was coming from the closet. Had he checked there earlier? Fool!

Suddenly the doors opened. Out stepped Horace Lechman.

"Mr. Kelly. Sorry to inconvenience you, however I am afraid that someone in this inn is intent on killing me."

"Tell me about it. They were shooting at me earlier in the spa."

"Oh, dear me. I am sorry about that. This all has nothing to do with you or Jeffrey, I assure you. I have my share of enemies. Ordinarily I wouldn't bring it up. However . . . under the circumstances . . . there are always those who are wont to attach various agendas and malevolence to those with wealth. My wealth, for the record, is my own. Achieved, by and large, honorably. Try and tell that to some of these characters."

David found his voice. "Are you suggesting that getting shot at is a regular occurrence for you?"

"Well, no. It isn't. However, I must say the shooter could work for any one of a number of less than savory cartels. In business, there is always a winner and always a loser. I have enjoyed many wins. That means . . ." Horace's voice trailed off, his meaning clear.

"Now then, perhaps you noticed my driver when he brought you in . . . 'Sensei.' He's actually my bodyguard. Knows how to kill a man about a hundred different ways. I need for you to make your way outside and have him pick me up around back. I'll take my leave through your window here, if it's all the same to you. Tell Jeffrey I have removed myself both for my own and your security. Things will calm down tomorrow, I predict, and then you will take my other plane which is, at present, enroute to pick you and Jeffrey up tomorrow."

"What about our ceremony? The signing?"

Lechman handed David a small object.

"Know what this is?"

"It's a 'hon.' Your personal ink stamp. They're used for signatures here in Japan."

"Very good. Very good, my lad. Now then, you take this, use it on the documents. It is legally binding, I can assure you. Give it back to me Stateside. Agreed?"

As Lechman began unlocking the window, David quickly made his way to the car and to 'Sensei.' When he returned to his room, Lechman had already left. He went about preparing things following Max's instructions. He piled furniture against the door and moved the futon away from the locked window. Then, holding tight to Lechman's 'hon,' he spent the wintry night in Japan's far North Country perfecting the skill of sleeping with his eyes wide open.

He was a legislative assistant, for Christ's sake. He never met the President. He wasn't destined for greatness, only paperwork. And he had no interest in flying high. As he was learning, those who fly high make for easier targets.

CHAPTER FIVE

Maryland Suburbs of Washington, D.C.

Stateside, it was blustery late evening in a wide-awake high-rise situated in a Maryland suburb just north of the nation's capital. The "Special Team," as they were known here, was wide awake, electronically tracking President Matthew Walker and his associates, recording hour after hour of digital tape, enhanced by the latest high-tech gadgetry to filter out unwanted background noises or to enhance them, depending on the tapers' needs.

And he knew it. Presidents for some years now had made their peace with security measures so draconian as to make them virtual prisoners during their tenures in office. President Clinton was said to refer to the White House as the most expensive federal prison facility in the nation. While presidents on occasion made light of their lack of privacy, they and their families were fully briefed on the alternatives – terrorist attacks, hostage situations, even World War III, triggered by a rogue nation, a ruthless infidel, or just some wacko with his own agenda. As ever, the current president was happy to have the United States' jackals on full alert at all times.

Walker had lusted after this steel cocoon for as long as he could remember, growing up in Tennessee. Something of a Presidential historian himself, he could recall myriad details associated with past residents of 1600 Pennsylvania Avenue -- Jackie's pillbox hats, Eisenhower's war record, Nixon's fall from grace. From each president, he had gleaned pointers for his own growing arsenal of political skills.

From Kennedy, he memorized the mannerisms and speech habits, as well as the sexual ones. From Nixon, he learned to develop a watchful paranoia that only one not-to-the-manor-born could truly appreciate.

From Carter, he learned the risks of turning the other cheek – especially in the high stakes world of national politics, the ultimate hardball game. From Clinton, a near contemporary, he learned to cover his tracks, to poll every statement, word and deed. He learned the importance of having a "War Room," to answer his critics promptly and forcefully.

From LBJ, who served his revenge up cold, he learned the art of the deal . . . that every man (or woman), had their price. He learned to use the advantages of his physical stature to tower over his adversaries, intimidating them by his nearness and size. And he never forgot Lyndon's maxim, "Nothing for nothing."

Oddly, after a while, the constant presence of Secret Service agents and the silent electronic monitors became familiar parts of their temporary 'home' as chief executives over the most powerful country on earth. The package was bountiful and disturbing all at once – from luxurious travel onboard Air Force One, trusted and respectful Filipino man-servants who looked after every possible personal detail, to the national press corps jackals ever on the prowl for fresh meat.

And, as with the wildly popular television Veritas shows that follow real people with 24-hour video-cams, recording their foibles and missteps, Presidents' surveillance after awhile became nothing more than 'business as usual,' known, but not necessarily heeded. Indeed, the protective custody into which a First Family was initiated upon election was so totally encompassing that one more photo, one more reel of tape, another camera shot became inconsequential.

Matt Walker on this evening, as on other Tuesdays when the First Lady visited her mother in New York City, was uttering his usual speech, the one reserved for married ladies of a certain age and blondeness with whom he was 'sharing a unique moment in history.'

"Who would guess that you could be like this in bed? You simply do not give off that sort of aura."

"This is something I have never done before. Why, Roger would never forgive me, if he found out."

"Nor, I dare say, contribute to my re-election campaign."

"No, I think that would be fair to say."

The President abruptly rose from the bed, drew a sheet over himself, then turned to tenderly cover his attractive companion with a blanket. He began dressing to leave.

"I enjoyed this. I enjoyed you. You know, Tuesdays are my time. So, let's see what we can make out of it, you and me. You'd be doing the nation a favor. My staff talks about me behind my back, you know."

"What do you mean?"

"Oh, they have surmised, young rascals that they are, that my romantic life ain't much, given the First Lady's preference for younger men."

"Matt! My God, I had no idea! Why are you still together then?"

"Ah, you know the electorate. Still want the Norman Rockwell family unit, even though a fair number of them can't say the same. So, how about it, sweetheart? Think you can take me on? For the sake of the country?"

Giggling, "Why Mr. President, are you suggesting an affair of state?"

"Now you think about it. There's my guy in the hall waiting, so I have to get on back. Stay here. Take your time leaving. Oh, and by the way, I left two tickets to Sunday's gala for you and Roger. Wear something in black. You know how I love 'ya in black, darlin'."

In due course, President Matthew Walker, 45th president of the United States of America, but by no means the first to cheat on his wife, left Room 1356 of the Washington Hotel just across the street from the Treasury Department, and overlooking the White House South Lawn. He exited by a back door, in no less imaginative a way than any other husband who also might have chosen to 'stay late at the office.'

"Rabbit Jumber is moving. Entering back elevator with Agent 24."

Matt Walker made his way through the hotel's kitchen to the back alleyway. The kitchen workers went about their business, eyes averted, heads down.

"Damn," he thought. "This one's special."

He had just learned that the soft blond fuzz on her face extended down over her lightly tanned shoulders and even over perfectly rounded breasts. He had learned that this was a natural blonde. Nature had bestowed this one with long legs, drenched in Chanel #5 that had wrapped themselves clean around his thighs. A man could get damned used to that sort of treatment. He climbed into his waiting car and picked up his car phone.

Punching 'Record,' he spoke. "Millie, please send Leila Harumi two dozen – make that one dozen. . ." -- two dozen would be obvious, he thought – "one dozen yellow roses. She and her husband have been so kind to my re-election campaign. Have the card read . . . (He faltered a moment as he thought up the perfect message, suggestive enough, yet one that, if intercepted, would raise no undue alarm) -- "Affairs of State are so much easier with your kind support. Look forward to seeing you both on Sunday." "And sign it 'Matt.'"

The leader of the free world had a second call to make that evening. One far more important. But here his instincts, those of a wily fox, kicked in. He recalled the "Special Unit." "Here's where you boys get off," he thought. "A little romance of an evening, just to let you see me with my guard down. Show's over now. Say goodnight. Go home to your little wives in Rockville."

Walker always enjoyed entering the upstairs den in the living quarters. The finest wood craftsman in the United States -- a Swedish fellow who normally outfitted the interiors of yachts – had built floor to ceiling bookshelves at his particular request to house the hundreds of books inhaled and then leather-bound by this intellectual president. And acoustics experts had outfitted the room for sound, in both directions as he was aware.

As he threw his coat to a waiting aide, he gave the final nod, an inclination of the head that signaled the end of a President's official day at last. Nuclear attacks, planes flying at the White House, untoward deaths, he was to be awakened. He thought with a chuckle, if a plane's headed for the Capitol dome, lemme sleep!

If the First Lady wished, she and she alone, could disturb his private time. She could barge right in with her latest decorating scheme for his consideration no matter the hour. Anyone else, for any other reason, would feel a wrath so unexpected and so severe, they would never again make the mistake of trespassing on this president.

With one exception.

Leon Barshevsky, Walker's long-time and trusted advisor. Leon could say or do anything, so trusted was the man many viewed as

Walker's Svengali. His was the flip side of the Commander in Chief, the side that could, let us say delicately, do the unthinkable, take out the garbage, operate in the shadows. Barshevsky had come out of the international community, rising through the ranks at the State Department.

He had been a military analyst, and an aide de camp to NATO leaders in Brussels. His family was old European money, making his government work a matter of belief rather than necessity. He had taken to America in a big way since he first arrived twenty years earlier. His family had purchased land in the hills above Santa Barbara. And he had set about working for the Party, to ensure that his values and holdings would be protected.

Leon was a citizen, but he was a 'nouveau citizen.' One might even call him a kind of 'designer citizen,' based on his unique take on democracy. He was in America for its opportunity, for its treatment of his family's wealth. Power was a good thing. He had watched as America had dominated the NATO alliance for years. Dominance suited this man to a "T." That is why he keyed on Matthew Walker. In him, he found a man as enamored of power in all its ramifications as he. Together, the men could do anything. So long as they remained in the power seats.

Walker came to depend on Barshevsky's can-do attitude. On his activism. On his way of circumventing the very bureaucracy Walker was charged with directing. He was, like Walker, a man who believed in the Bill of Rights, for himself. Inalienable rights for others? Less important. In Barshevsky's and Walker's world, the operating principle, "What's ours is ours and what's yours is negotiable," served well. It was the basis of their working relationship.

Each understood what the bottom line was. Neither felt the need to expound to the other about the 'right thing to do.' Because both knew instinctively what the 'right thing' was. There was never a question.

And so, Leon entered Walker's inner sanctum tonight at will, carrying two glasses of Cognac. As he handed one off, a nod of the head and a quick look from under his deeply hooded eyelids told Walker all he needed to know.

"Good evening, Leon?"

"Good evening, Mr. President."

"We are making progress then?"

"More than progress, sir. I would say that the group's agenda is in particularly sound shape this evening."

Walker walked to a framed photograph of himself being sworn in as President of the United States. Only one man standing within the frame was of equal height. Horace Lechman. Walker spoke. "Fine looking man. Strong. Like a father to me."

Leon glanced at the much-studied photograph. "Yes sir. A fine man. A toast then?"

Walker lifted his Cognac. "To old friends."

Leon responded, "Indeed, old friends. Indeed."

The two men stood staring into the fire for awhile as they finished their drinks. Then Walker held out his hand. "Got something for me?" Leon reached into a pocket and withdrew a cassette tape. The President proceeded to unreel the tape onto the floor. "Probably a mistake. Let's not have two." With that, Leon bent down, picked up the spent tape, and cast it into the fire. The two men stood together watching it burn. Only after every piece of tape had turned to ashes did they turn back to the drink cart.

CHAPTER SIX

Airfield, Mellon Estate, Middleburg, Virginia

The big Lechman jet was circling to land as both David and Layton struggled with the news they had received six hours earlier. Horace Lechman was missing and presumed dead after his 50-foot motor sailor went down in a violent thunderstorm on Chesapeake Bay.

But how could that be? They were just with the man less than twenty-four hours ago. Sometimes the time between life and death can be fifteen minutes. Just fifteen minutes.

Peering out the window of the wood-paneled aircraft, David watched as a herd of priceless thoroughbred horses, spooked by the jet engines, ran across the perfectly manicured fields, tails flying in the wind. Besides the chestnut of the horses, there were two other colors below – the rich green of the Virginia countryside and the white of mile upon mile of perfectly maintained farm-land fences.

David worked to make sense of the last few days – so much had happened, it seemed like he had been away from Washington for a lifetime. Here he was, seated in a billionaire's plane. About to ride in his black limousine. And be greeted by the man's fresh widow at his Middleburg estate.

But, how much of it was really true? Had a billionaire presidential donor really been hiding in David's closet? Or had the past forty-eight hours instead only been the result of David's over-active imagination? A way for him to avoid his own life?

Catching a glimpse of Layton's face gave David his answer. They were about to land on a private jet landing strip in the center of Virginia's Hunt Country to visit a grieving widow. It was real alright. David needed to concentrate on getting through the present. The next several hours would be murder, he thought.

Death. For some, it came as relief. For Horace Lechman, and his wife Sybil, as David would soon learn, it came as heart wrenching tragedy. One look at the woman as they drove up, and one knew for sure it wasn't about the money. To be sure, Sybil had enjoyed improving economic status as a result of several marriages to increasingly wealthy men. But unless this woman was one helluva good actress, she had just lost part of herself.

The woman standing before them in perfectly tailored lavender suit, holding a martini in one hand and a Yorkshire Terrier in the other, was a wreck. How could he tell? David noted the resolute set of her shoulders. The lack of tears. The perfect makeup. On some, these might have signaled an uncaring coldness. But Sybil was not your typical widow. Because, in her own eyes, she wasn't actually a widow.

Not yet.

She was certain, verily certain, that Horace was not gone. He was yet to be retrieved magically off Gibson Island. Clever man. He had taken refuge under a tree. He had fallen asleep. Didn't hear the helicopters searching him out. Was surprised at everyone's fuss. Yes, that was it. He would be home soon. In the meantime, it was so good of her dear friend, Jeffrey Layton to stop by.

She bustled about to impress David being the fine hostess that she was. For all the world, she was intent that he have a comfortable seat. Be served a bowl of cook's fresh chicken soup. Be included in the conversation, even though it was of a personal nature, and he was nothing more than a ride-along.

She inquired as to his comfort during the flight. Worried that he might require a lap robe on the chilly sun porch. Through all of these hostess acts, Layton watched and waited. David could tell he was biding his time until he would need to help his friend deal with heavier issues. Issues like death. Trust accounts. Funerals. Solitude.

As David took his leave . . . the Secretary was staying over . . . he once again fell into his normal state of depression. Telling himself it wasn't about him, that everything wasn't about him, nevertheless, he couldn't help wondering if he were killed suddenly whether there would be a woman there for him as grief stricken as Sybil was about her Horace.

Such love at any age was something to see. No, not see. Feel. Because all the way back to town, David felt caught in the grip of Sybil Lechman. The sixtyish woman at the horse farm. With her silly little dog and her martinis.

"Ernie Fields, his ass," he thought once again.

CHAPTER SEVEN

Home at Last

Safely home, David checked his messages. The first was from Max Berfield: "Hey there, James Bond. So what happened? Were 'ya killed? If so, lemme know will 'ya? Need to update my Christmas card list."

Next up was Julie: "David. I forgot to give you the boys' school pictures when you were here. So, I guess I'll just put them in the mail to you . . .say, wasn't that man who's missing supposed to be with you in Japan? I was just wondering . . ."

"Yeh, me too," he thought.

Finally, there was a message from Jeffrey Layton.

"Uh, David. You home yet? Guess not. Listen, you don't need to mention my whereabouts to anyone – wouldn't want the ball and chain catching wind – I plan to stay here one more day. As I am sure you have heard by now, Horace Lechman's been officially declared, they found some remains. Sad thing. Sad, sad thing. Matt's due by here tomorrow – apparently the divers found some personal items in the Bay, and he will be delivering them in person to Mrs. Lechman.

Another thing. He wants to see me in the Oval Tuesday morning, at ten a.m. along with his Schnauzer, Barshevsky. Plan on meeting me over there, sit outside, see what you can pick up – troop movements, gossip, the usual. Then maybe we can grab a bite after. Remember, mum's the word about my location."

David switched on the TV. Lechman's confirmed death was all over cable news. "I'll be damned," he muttered to no one in particular. He had started doing that a lot lately, living alone. He talked to himself and even held entire conversations with his beloved tropical fish, swimming along in their wall-sized tank. The swimmers, plus floor to ceiling books and a fireplace combined to make this condominium more than a temporary resting place. David had made sure that it was home. His home. Peaceful and welcoming.

He entered his kitchen – outfitted for the gourmet cook that he was. A second fireplace set waist-high in the corner of the dining nook had been an add-on after he had spent a particularly rainy day in Carmel on Monterey Bay. There, despite the winter chill, every store, no matter how small, featured a welcoming wood-burning fireplace that distributed heat generously to damp visitors. David hurried to his balcony to gather up wood for his kitchen fireplace. He located a half-empty bottle of wine in the refrigerator. After building a fire, he settled into a wing-back chair nearby.

Someone was knocking on his front door. It was the doorman bringing him his mail.

"Mr. Kelly, is your phone working alright now?"

"Yeh, why do you ask?"

"A repairman was by while you were out of town. Said he fixed it for you."

"A phone man."

"Yes. That's right. Phone man. Well, uh, Mr. Kelly, welcome home, and you have a good evening now."

David opened the hall credenza for tip money. He handed the doorman a five and thanked him.

Pouring another glass of wine for himself, he picked up the phone receiver and listened. Just a dial tone. Normal dial tone.

"Huh," he thought.

He tried it again. Nothing. No clicking noises. No heavy breathing. He had no energy to take it further. Probably a mistake. A simple mistake. Like everything else lately. Being shot at? Mistake. Divorce? Mistake. Lechman's accident? Mistake.

Slowly his head nodded, the fire crackled away, and his fish, oblivious to it all, swam happily along. Tomorrow was another day.

CHAPTER EIGHT

David sleep-walked his way through Monday, Presidents' Day. He arose late, fixed a spectacular breakfast, and read the Washington and New York papers from cover-to-cover. The extensive news coverage concerning Lechman's death was not unexpected, given the man's wealth and stature. Accolade after accolade was offered by scions of government and industry. The man had touched many lives that was clear.

Tabloid treatments showed a steady parade of limousines making their way up the long drive of the Lechman estate as those closest to the family, including the President, arrived to pay their respects. No sign of the widow so far. That did not stop the speculation, however. About the size of the estate. Her relations with his children. How many husbands she had had in her expanding matrimonial career. In short, the sniping had begun. Before the funeral.

Inhaling the coverage, David thought he might learn more about Horace Lechman's business dealings, possibly why someone wanted him dead. His drowning was an accident, right?

Clueless, he searched the papers for any information that might help explain events in the past forty-eight hours. He read all about the lightning strike, the fire onboard, the sinking of the luxurious motor sailor. He also read any news about U.S. overseas development projects. About Matt Walker's aggressive wilderness preservation program. And he searched for news having to do with Japan. An item about stray gunmen shooting at tourists in Hokkaido would be helpful, he thought wryly.

One headline caught his eye: "Japan's UniStar Buying U.S. Battleship in Latest Shipping Deal." He read on: "The UniStar Group said yesterday that it had agreed to acquire the U.S. Battleship Kansas from the United States government, saving another former U.S. battleship from reclamation. The ship was sold to the Japanese conglomerate for about $48 million, the fifth ship to be purchased by UniStar in the past year."

The article pointed out that Japan, possessing no military fleet of its own, would use the ship for its expanding trade shipments.

"Huh. Nothing."

David gathered up the pile of newspapers and delivered them to the building's trash room. He returned to his desk and began making out a grocery list for the veal shanks with mushrooms he would make for dinner. He had just added "1 pound small cremini mushrooms . . ." to his list, when it hit him.

UniStar. Of course. He quickly located his suitcase. Common traveling thief that he was, he had stolen a towel from the hotel. Pulling it out, he noted the monogram – a black circle with red star inside. Of course, UniStar.

Meaning, David scolded himself, absolutely nothing. So, what if an international corporation owned swank hotels and shipping companies? No news there. So, what if Horace Lechman had contracted with them to build a casino in Japan, wouldn't he make a profit? . . . so, what if President Walker had committed U.S. funds to saving resource-rich land on Japan's northern island, wasn't that just good diplomacy? . . . Just because Secretary Layton had dragged him off to the deal signing . . . so, fucking what?!

His mind continued on automatic pilot: So, what if Horace Lechman met with an untimely death? So, what if there were a wintry storm on the Bay? So, what if David ducked a few gunshots clearly meant for someone else? So, what if an over-zealous phone repairman entered his home while he was away? So, what if a Japanese corporation were doing business with America? Happened all the time.

Nothing. He got nothing. Except a headache. Time for a glass of wine. Wasn't it five o'clock somewhere on the planet?!

CHAPTER NINE

Otaru, on Hokkaido's north coast

A man wearing full toxic hazard suit exited his truck inside the tall gates of a large industrial complex located on Japan's northernmost coast. From the banks of the city of Otaru, one could see Russia's Sakhalin Islands on a clear day. Siberian winds swept the area with frigid temperatures year around.

The driver carried a clipboard as he approached the guard shack of this highly secure facility. Cameras and watch towers monitored all movements in and around the area. He carefully unzipped an external pocket to remove his company I.D. He unsnapped his face mask for the retinal identification scanner and placed thumb prints on a horizontal glass screen for further verification.

Satisfied, the guard signed his papers and motioned the driver to proceed. As the driver climbed back into his cab, the guard approached him and motioned for him to unroll the window. He handed up a leather pouch. On its side was a decal. It was a round black circle with red star inside. The driver reached for the pouch. Finally, as the gates swung open, the driver, his cargo and the pouch left the premises. Bound for . . .

CHAPTER TEN

Washington, D.C.

"White House Day" dawned unseasonably warm with a sharp sun etching winter's trees in stark relief. 'Season-Affect-Disordered' Washingtonians took to the jogging trails en masse to take advantage of the warm weather. David Kelly was due at the White House by ten, a big day by anyone's standards.

First, however, he joined the rest of the city on a crowded running trail in Rock Creek Park, a wilderness park located in the heart of the city. With the park's connection to the Blue Ridge Mountains, all manner of wild animals dwelt side-by-side with the elite of the nation's capital, resulting in occasional unexpected interactions: one morning, a black bear was found foraging on the White House grounds, having missed his turn at Pennsylvania Avenue, failing to secure the proper visitor's entry pass.

David needed to work the kinks from his travel-weary body that had been off-schedule and out of kilter lately. Gradually, endorphins kicked in, and he could feel himself returning to his former, more optimistic self.

"Thank God," he thought. "Maybe I'm not nuts, after all."

Approaching the forty-five-minute point of his run, he rounded a sharp turn high above Georgetown's fabled 'P Street Beach.' As a crowd of people converged at the curve, David found himself suddenly tangled with other runners. A hot-shot biker on a cell phone seemed to have caused the human pile-up. At the bottom of the stack, David caught sight of the long red braid of some poor woman at the bottom.

As he untangled himself, and helped others to their feet, David reacted to the arrogant man on the bike, who made no effort to assist anyone, and rode off. Then he glanced nervously at his watch – "I have to be at the White House," he thought, importantly. "I have no time for this."

Somewhere inside this stressed and preoccupied policy lobbyist, however, another reaction took hold. In the commotion of various pairs of arms and legs righting themselves, he noted the freckles running across the bridge of her nose. Then saw the red braid that extended to her waist, shining in the winter sun. And green eyes the exact shade of Lake Tahoe in summer.

As David's long-dormant bells and whistles went off, another man helped her to her feet, encouraging her to lean on him as she limped away. All David could do was stand there staring after her, as awkwardly as any man in love could. Regions of his body reminded him of what a woman could do. A certain woman. The one woman in the universe. He used to think that was Julie. Well, he was wrong. Clearly wrong. There was one other. And she had just left.

Not one to be sidetracked by details, such as how or where they might ever meet again in a city of umpteen million people, David fairly skipped for joy. He had seen her. The rest was just details. Because she existed.

Here.

In Washington.

"Dream Girl."

CHAPTER ELEVEN

David had been to the White House four times in his life. Exactly four. Visits to the White House, like remembering the day Kennedy was shot, or where one was on 9-11, were memorable. So far as he could tell, there was no particular reason for him to be at the White House, except as a visible member of "Team Layton."

He was not invited into the room, but merely to hover outside it. His instructions were to proceed directly to the Oval Office and wait for Secretary Layton. Of David's visits to the mansion, this one, "Number Five," was his first to the Oval Office.

He knew that in the future, his version of today's events would place him inside participating in the meeting, not waiting outside the double doors, like some flunky. Failure to embellish the story would be a virtual denial of every political instinct David had developed over the years. While he was generally honest and direct about most things, part of his DNA would always test positive for "Potomac Fever," a localized condition whose symptoms included an obsession with the news, an arcane knowledge of congressional committee assignments, and need for access to those in positions of power.

As he was being checked in, David once again was struck by the incongruous peacefulness of the big house. At the world's power epicenter were potted palms and Chinese vases full of fresh flowers atop antique cherry desks. Thick Annapolis-blue carpeting dampened sounds, and the hum of activity was serene, unlike any business office David had known. Soft lamp lighting replaced the usual glare of office fluorescent, and phones were turned down low, daring only occasional melodic notes to announce calls.

Gazing down upon this elegant environment and those who walked its long, wide halls, were the home's former residents, men who had guided the nation to today. Kelly noticed their slightly bemused expressions and wondered if all artists painted portraits in this way, or if instead, the subjects shared a secret. Something they wanted to share but could not. A secret perhaps in common with each other, but not for the citizenry. Were they not, after all, members of one of the most exclusive men's clubs in the world?

A young intern, with a large photo I.D. importantly hanging around his neck, escorted David to the Oval Office area. He refused to leave his side until David had been officially passed on to a presidential secretary.

In short order, the President's personal secretary, Millie Avignel, had taken his coat and directed Kelly to a seat near the big doors to the office. A Philippine man dressed in crisp white Nehru jacket placed a silver tray beside him bearing hot coffee, real cream in a pitcher, sugar and a packet of M&M candies with the Presidential seal on them.

The scene could not have been farther removed from David's own paper-strewn government office with spent Styrofoam coffee cups perched on stacks of reports. His own M&Ms, he noted wryly, had no special logos. They came to him straight from the canteen located in the back hall.

Two members of the Secret Service stood watch nearby. They looked bored, he noted. As he took a sip of the satisfying brew, Kelly took in his surroundings. It was not every day that one was able to observe the inner workings of the White House.

"God damn it all to Hell, Jeffrey!"

The President's distinctive voice boomed straight through the walls of his office. A loud crash followed – it sounded to Kelly like a piece of furniture had just hit the wall.

The two agents sprang into action. Racing by David, they knocked over his coffee table as they reached for their service revolvers. The men were from the top echelon of the Secret Service, assigned directly to the Presidential Personal Detail. As such, they were trained to handle terrorists, bomb threats, and whack-job citizens. Their specialty was the unexpected. They were tough real life action figures, who could kill with their bare hands if the occasion called for it.

But someone tougher had beaten them to the door. Someone with superior reaction time. Someone whose resolve was greater, whose way could not be breached. Milly Avignel stood in front of the great doors, arms akimbo. Her look of warning would have stopped charging Rottweilers dead in their tracks. This diminutive woman in grey wool suit had dealt with world leaders for most of her career. She guarded the President on a daily basis from competitive staffers and visitors vying for access.

Secret Service agents were no problem for Milly Avignel. Silently, she faced down the men and their drawn guns. Sheepishly, the two backed off and returned to their posts. Their tension, however, remained palpable, and like the guard dogs they were, their eyes stayed riveted on the double doors.

The waiter returned, calmly cleaned the spilt coffee and replaced the setting as though nothing untoward had happened. Kelly noticed the man forgot to replace his M&Ms. He laughed at the whole scene and his own thoughts. Then the office grew still again. Above the soft hum of office activity, David became acutely aware of a ticking grandfather clock in a hallway.

"What had just happened here?" he wondered. "Besides Layton and the President, who was in the meeting? Leon Barshevsky? Was this normal Matt Walker behavior?"

He glanced at his watch. The meeting seemed to go on forever.

After twenty minutes had passed, a buzzer sounded on Milly's desk. She rose and quickly crossed to the doors, giving David and the guards a stern glance on her way by. The doors opened, and out walked Jeffrey Layton, smiling expansively. Behind him, David could glimpse the President seated at his desk already on the phone.

Leon Barshevsky was replacing a large wingback chair from where it had landed to its rightful place to one side of the desk. Both men pointedly ignored the Secretary's departure. The meeting clearly was over.

The Secretary was especially charming around the ladies. David had seen him in action before. Now, he watched in amazement as he bade Millie goodbye. A woman who met smooth politicians all day long was nevertheless clearly flattered by the Secretary's attention.

Layton had an Old-World courtliness about him that trumped men decades younger every time. You would have thought he had all the time in the world and that the only person of interest to him at this point was Milly Avignel.

'Give the Secretary your best. You always have.'

David took a long look at Layton talking with Millie. He always gave him his best. How long had he been with the man? Twenty? No, twenty-three years? Since he was governor. Not just 'a' governor. 'The' governor. A nationally, even internationally, respected politician who had carved out environmental salvation and resource restoration as his own personal missions in life.

As a young idealistic lawyer, David was honored to work for the intellectual politician. Jeffrey Layton's own father had once served as governor of New Mexico, following the Udall legacy back in the democratic "machine" days. Seeing rough and tumble politics up close growing up, the younger Layton headed out for a monastery, there to take the vow of silence for more than a year. He meditated. He thought good thoughts. Growing bored with the devout life, headed back down the hill, back to the rough and tumble contact sport of politics.

David liked the way Layton wore black turtleneck sweaters and smoked a pipe. Dress up for the scholarly politician then consisted of throwing an expensive tweed jacket over the black uniform. Bolstered by family money, not to mention family name, Layton easily won election after election, becoming the most innovative governor in Washington state history.

For his devotion to trying new solutions, some derided him. For a brief moment in time, when he toyed with a presidential run, the national media, conformist jackals that they were, jumped all over him. They seemed only too glad to carry opposition slogans and epithets into any story about the independent Pacific Northwesterner. He bowed out of national politics with some relief. Who needed it?

Years passed, Layton's reputation and good deeds grew. Finally, the current president, realizing the value of the environment and resource restoration, tapped Layton to head up his new agency, the Department of Resource Development. At the outset, he gave Layton his head. Let him run things. Gradually, however, the President and the President's men intervened. They had Layton right where they wanted him now. Trapped between his strong ethics and a partisan hard place. How long would it take this intellectual recruit to chew through his ropes and get away?

David could tell there had been a sea change lately. What he could not yet see was in what direction. On the surface, all appeared calm. But an increasingly fidgety Layton, oddly changing legislative directives, and a White House demanding more and more proof, and more paperwork, told him something was up. But what?

David snapped out of his reverie as Layton turned to him. He gave him a sharp uncharacteristic slap on the back; the only sign things weren't right.

"Well, there's the boy. Right on time. What say we make our way on out to lunch? How about a nice pastrami sandwich? With some German beer to wash it down . . . . so, it doesn't get stuck in our craws . . ."

With the suggestion, Layton took off at a brisk clip and did not speak again until both were seated inside his chauffeured Town Car.

As the car passed through the anti-terrorism "Jersey Barriers" set along the White House perimeter, they saw a street woman pushing a shopping cart with a little dog walking along beside her. Layton observed, "Now will you just look at that poor woman? How on earth, do you suppose, a woman gets herself in that kinda shape?"

"Maybe she had a husband once. A family. A home. All the usual, normal things. Maybe she drove her sons to soccer practice several days a week. Cooked a chicken dinner for the family on Sundays. And then, something just . . . happened. To take it all away . . ."

For the first time that day, Layton took a close look at his aide. "We aren't only talking about that woman, now are we. Eh?"

"I just mean things aren't always what they seem."

"Oh, ho! Isn't that the truth?! Now then, we'll be fine once we make our way to the New York Deli."

They rode in silence for a while. David watched as a bicycle courier careened around the car, barely missed them, and raced off through traffic. What would the everyday person think if they knew their president had just thrown a chair across the Oval Office? Was that normal behavior? For that matter, what was normal behavior? Damned if he knew anymore.

David slumped down in his seat as Layton took a look at his newspaper. Layton sensed David's mood. That was one of several things that set him apart from the common, run-of-the-mill politician in Washington – he noticed people. And he wanted to help. He always wanted to help.

"Now then, Mr. Deputy Assistant Secretary. Let me tell you something. I know, I know. You're dying to ask. But believe me when I say I am doing you a favor not saying. Suffice it to say some people aren't what they appear either."

"Son of a bitch! Now then, we'll be fine. We just keep on doing America's business. Remember why we are here. Remind me later, we need to work on that Alaskan Wilderness Report – for the Southern Prince."

David knew Layton's little sayings. 'Southern Prince' was shorthand he increasingly used for Matthew Walker.

The Secretary leaned back and caught a song playing on the driver's radio.

"That's from 'The Sound of Music.' The wife and I watched it again on the TV last night. Wonderful story. A family, threatened by the Nazi's. Walks right outta the country. What courage. What wonderful courage. Given the situation, would we do the same? I wonder."

A block and a half back in traffic, a black Chevy suburban with darkened windows followed the Town Car. The passenger held a small antenna trained on the other car.

"Nothing. They're talking about some movie."

"Let's head on back then."

With that, the big dark Chevy turned down an alleyway and drove several blocks to a parking garage. The driver waved a parking pass at the attendant and made his way to the lowest level, passing many open spaces along the way. At the bottom, he turned into a parking spot marked 'Handicapped' next to a fence that appeared to be housing the building's ventilation system.

Touching a bottom on the sun visor, the wall in front of the car lifted up, making room for the car to pass through. Once the car was safely inside, the wall re-closed, leaving no trace of the two men or their vehicle. They were now back at their 'office.'

Back at the New York Deli, several diners recognized Secretary Layton but left the two men to enjoy their lunch in peace. As he wiped the thick granular mustard from his chin, David thought that at least one could get a decent pastrami on rye in Washington.

CHAPTER TWELVE

Maryland Suburbs of Washington, D.C.

"God damn it all to Hell, Jeffrey!"

The unmistakable voice of the Commander in Chief laid down its characteristic tracings on the security audio tape. The analyst had heard many similar remarks on this job. There were specific guidelines that kicked his analysis to another level. Swearing was not one of them. Hidden away from the electorate, language in the Oval Office got pretty racy. Also, racist, bigoted and chauvinistic. Political correctness was left at the North Lawn portico as the nation's larger issues got resolved.

The sound of a chair being pitched against the wall – along with movement sensor tracings that confirmed the hit – was an activity under the guidelines that moved the electronic monitoring activity up a notch. There was even a graph somewhere of this president's temper tantrums. As strange as it might seem, this particular presidential outlet of energy – throwing office furniture – had taken place in the past.

One might be safe in assuming that any person willing to accept the position of President by definition is a bit mad. Add to that an outsized ego, a history of having things one's own way, with everyone within spitting distance at one's beck and call, and you have conditions that are not exactly conducive to balance and sensitivity to the needs of others. Quite the opposite.

And that is why presidents are watched closely. Their behavior and reactions are monitored. Besides the much-publicized physical exams at Bethesda Naval Hospital, more discreet electronic tracings also are kept and analyzed on a continuous basis throughout the man's time in office.

It is only a myth that America's president is independent. In reality he is subject to careful assessments by those in charge of such things. After all, the nation would not be safe if its leader were to go off his rocker and initiate irrational actions, including military, to suit his own needs.

And who determines 'normal'?

They do.

And so, on this day, a report was made to the file. The outburst was added to his graph. Later the graph would be compared with the President's blood pressure medicine dosage, with whether or not "Mrs. President" were in town, and with the time interval since the last such outburst. The book was up-dated. The event was noted. Somewhere in the government.

CHAPTER THIRTEEN

It was past eight o'clock when David finally made his way home. His afternoon, post-pastrami sandwich, had been spent hunkered down over his desk pouring over reports and draft legislative language. Being out of town, flying off to Japan, jetting into Middleburg to pay calls on wealthy widows, while interesting, did nothing to complete David's agenda on time and convincingly.

It was the people's business, saving wilderness areas for the next generations. Say what you will about Matthew Walker -- and God knows, many did -- the man saw the long view. He had vision. And David was happy to serve as his implementer in that noble endeavor.

Tonight, David was too tired for gourmet treats. So, he microwaved an Idaho potato, grated some Tillamook cheddar on top. He grilled a piece of salmon, poured his first glass of wine of the evening, and settled down to simple, but delicious fare. The Carmel fireplace was geared up, and a third glass of wine was being poured when the phone rang.

"Let the machine get it," he muttered to himself, even as he rose from his chair.

As he picked up, there was a brief pause, then a click, before the caller spoke.

"David. Hello, this is Monica. Remember me?"

Remember her? Who could forget the blonde soap opera star with stunning figure and baby-breath voice?! He had met the beautiful young woman at a reception on Capitol Hill. She had been testifying before a Senate committee on the dangers of cleaning fluids to children with cancer.

Like so many in the entertainment industry, she was fascinated with political Washington, and high as a kite from her brief exposure on the 'expert panel' that addressed a Senate health committee that day. David carefully answered her questions about how to influence legislation and continued his tutorial at lunch the next day before she flew back to New York.

While he was flattered by her attention, he knew he was nothing more to her than an information source. Given her womanly and sweet nature directed to a man lately starved for such company, he viewed her call with unexpected pleasure.

"Yes, of course. Monica Waters. How are you?"

"Busy. Very busy. My character has been in the hospital lately. Her boyfriend beat her up because she accidentally burned his house down . . . oh, you don't want to know about all that. Why I am calling is because I have a week's hiatus while she gets well again, so I thought I might come down to Washington. I just wanted to ask you to dinner . . ."

"Geez Louise," David thought. Could his life get any stranger? But he answered directly.

"Of course. Sounds good. I have a pretty clear calendar next week, so just give me a call when you get into town. I know a couple of nice places you might enjoy."

The actress rang off, promising to call when she arrived. She was planning on staying at the Hay Adams Hotel. Nice choice, he thought. Oddly, his thoughts turned to his friend, Max Berfield. Max would be pleased by this development, he thought. Max had been after him to get out more. He wanted his friend to date. To reap the benefits of the divorce, even as he went home to his wife and four children night after night.

David Kelly was his fantasy life. And lately, according to Max, David had been falling down on the job. If only for Max's well-being, David thought, dinner with Monica would be a good thing. Hell, it wouldn't hurt David either! Suddenly, the Wilderness legislation seemed less important.

CHAPTER FOURTEEN

Wyoming

The 42nd[th] President of the United States would be known as "The Wilderness President." Already successful in saving thousands of acres of pristine wilderness area in Wyoming from rapacious corporate interests, he was now crafting a plan to do the same in the fiftieth state.

Alaska would be his legacy. Even as 'end of oil' activists called for drilling in Alaska, he asked his Secretary of Development to be his point man in pushing his Alaska Wilderness bill through the Congress.

But first, there was some unfinished business to attend to. Park officials in the Wyoming National Forest were talking to environmentalists and others about some disturbing findings in these federal lands. They reported shocking examples of 'monster babies,' animals born without brains, or with their intestines outside their bodies, or with their nose where their eyes should be.

According to one park ranger quoted in a local newspaper, "We have experienced seven times the normal number of observed birth defects and newborn cancers in the past two years in park animals."

A retired nuclear physicist living in the area read the news report with unusual interest. During his active career, he had specialized in aberrant life forms resulting from exposure to nuclear materials. He visited the park, was shown the photographs, and sent some of them along to a former colleague at a federal research lab located in the nation's capital.

While the deformities seemed consistent with exposure to depleted uranium known as 'DU,' the scientist was unaware of the presence of uranium near the park. 'DU,' 'Uranium 238,' had a half-life estimated at over four billion years. It was highly unlikely that there could be any connection. Not here. Not in the nation's park system. Not where the Wilderness President's legacy got its start.

To make certain of that, presidential aide Leon Barshevsky placed a few strategic phone calls . . . to the director of the Washington research lab . . . to the head of the National Park Service . . . and a few others. Following the discussions, the scientist and park rangers had nothing further to say on the subject.

There were no further articles in the local newspaper. In due time, environmentalists stood down following publication of an article in the prestigious World Nature Organization's journal, debunking reports as nothing more than tabloid hoaxes.

In this way, old news remained where old news belongs.

In the dustbin of time.

CHAPTER FIFTEEN

David took a lunch break with Max, his Special Forces turned war correspondent friend, at Washington's venerable watering hole, the Monocle. Located in a townhouse near Senate office buildings, a short walk from Union Station, the Monocle was 'action central' for Washington insiders.

Both men hailed from the Pac Northwest. As a result, they possessed a matter-of-fact western attitude, questioning authority, and reading between the lines as they went about their work on the Hill.

From that base, their friendship had lasted more than twenty years, surviving relationships, divorces and other trials. The men's trust level in each other ran high. One experience, however, in all their years had never come up.

Murder.

Max led off.

"You came pretty close to being removed from my Christmas card list!"

"Don't remind me."

"So, what's the deal? You reading too many detective novels?"

David took a sip of the wine Max had ordered.

"I . . . have . . . absolutely no idea, Max. Maybe so. One minute I was in the hot tub . . . hey, even though I have never been in combat like you, I think I know the sound of gunfire. . . plus, the bullets were tearing up the water right next to me!"

Max replied, "It is a pretty distinctive sound. Sure it wasn't the local Ainu Indians playing cops and robbers outside?"

"Let's drop it. I have no idea. And, as they say, I'd like to just move on."

Max sighed. "Okay. It's your funeral. But let me know if anything else funny happens . . ."

"What d'ya mean 'funny'?

"Oh, you know, the usual: strange men following you around. . . phone taps . . . odd looking mail . . ."

"And become as paranoid as you, Max?"

"Listen, there's paranoia and there's awareness. Sometimes the one resembles the other. You know how you can tell the difference, don't you?"

"How?"

"With one, you wind up dead."

"Oh jeez, thanks a lot. Can we change the subject? Please?!"

Max recalled David's earlier phone call. His news about some girl in the park.

"So, tell me about that girl in the park yesterday. Get her name?"

David already had assigned 'Dream Girl' to another area of his consciousness. She was not up for discussion. She existed. He would find her. He would marry her. They would live on his new liveaboard. But he had no desire to detail his plans for Max. They were too personal, even for him.

He changed the subject.

"The man's really tense lately. I think he's mixed up in some sort of secret deal with Walker . . ."

Max answered. "He is a cabinet member. Secret's the name of the game at that level. So, what?"

David continued his disjointed thoughts: "Met Sybil . . ."

"Who?"

"You know, Horace Lechman. His widow -- Sybil. Nice lady. I think there might be something going on with her and Layton . . ."

"Again, so what?"

David shrugged his shoulders, "It's just interesting. I mean, to see two people in their seventies . . . I have to admit, seeing them together made me a little jealous. I mean, who do I have? My fish?"

Max began playing an imitation violin. "Poor David. What about that actress? Sounds like a date to me."

"Next week. But, Max, you know . . ."

"Yeh, life's tough. Having dinner with a blonde bombshell. Flying off to Japan on private jets. Did you see Julie in Seattle?"

"We tried talking. The usual routine. Missed Kenny again." Abruptly, Kelly raised a clenched fist, bringing it full force on the white tablecloth, sending forks flying to the floor. Diners nearby turned in his direction. "Damn it all!"

Max's tone softened, "Easy now. I know you, don't forget. So, you can drop the act."

"Act, Max?"

"You know damned well what happened. Nobody's to blame here. Not you. Not Julie. She just didn't like Washington. Can't say I blame her."

"Huh." Kelly's head nodded, and he reached for his glass of wine.

"You know I have a theory. . ."

"Theories, theories . . ."

"Whenever you talk about your life – especially your job – lately, it comes out negative. Then there's the matter of your mid-life crisis. You're overdue, you know."

David sipped his drink, then took a long gulp. "Bullshit, Max. That's psychological pap . . . hey, but I think I might be an alcoholic . . ."

"I've seen a few of those in my day, and I am sorry to have to tell you this, but you don't make the grade . . . denial's not just a river in Egypt, you know."

"What's that supposed to mean?"

Max waved his arm, "I see a red sports car in your future. Because when you blow, buddy, you're gonna go big. Hell, you already have one of the classic symptoms, dating a blond soap opera actress . . ."

" . . . not dating . . ."

"What do you call it then?"

David had had enough, "None of your damned business comes to mind."

Max backed off. "Well, it's a start. Hey, listen, who the hell knows what they're doing anyway? Everyone's faking it. That's for sure. Especially in this town! So, tell me, how was Layton's meeting with Walker?"

"I think it was some sort of debriefing on the trip. 'Course, Lechman's money's probably dried up on Japan . . . unless he had it in his will or something . . . which I kind of doubt . . .Speaking of which, you ever heard of a company name of 'UniStar'?"

Max nodded his head in the negative.

"Their logo's a black circle with a red star in the middle. I seem to be seeing it everywhere lately. There's this pouch Layton's taken to carrying around – I've seen it in his open briefcase in the car . . ." Realizing he might be saying too much, even to Max, David abruptly changed course . . . "So, he – Layton – calls Walker 'the Southern Prince' – things are eroding, that's for sure. Wonder how long I have in this job."

"There is an antidote to all of this, David. Called a life. Remember? Recall 'happy' for me. That's it. Your face looks better already. And you know that actress – what d'ya say her name was . . .?"

"Monica. Waters."

" . . . Monica. She is an excellent place to start."

"Uh-huh."

Max continued. "You know what your problem is – you look down your nose at people who are simply happy."

"You mean simple people who are happy, don't you Max?"

"You might want to try it. Life's short, buddy."

David answered his friend. "I'm fine. Really. Hey, did you get a load of that brunette who just walked in? Know her?"

"I'm not going to press this. But you know I'm here for you. Hell, I'll feel your pain."

"Anyone ever tell you you're nuts?"

"Just like sailing, buddy. Wind changes direction, you make a course correction."

As the two men finished their lunch, the room took on a late afternoon glow. One of Washington's violent thunderstorms was positioning itself directly overhead. The sky turned charcoal black. The wind picked up as the men hailed a cab. David paused on the street corner as Max climbed into the car.

"You go on without me. Think I'm going to walk back to the office."

Max replied, "In this weather. Come on, ride with me."

"I'll be fine, Max. I'll head on down to Union Station. There's a book I want to buy anyway. I'll call you this week-end. Maybe we can hit a few balls if the weather cooperates."

"Suit yourself," Max responded as the car door swung closed. David pulled his raincoat tighter across his chest and turned into the park. He noted a security guard making a bomb check on the undercarriage of a car headed to the Russell Senate Office Building. It's like a war zone, he noted. Then a strong gust of wind cleared his head, making him think of Puget Sound. He thought of tacking in a strong wind, then, the wind to his back, made his way 'wing-on-wing' down-hill to the train station.

Once inside, with a crowd of travelers and shoppers, his thoughts again became jumbled. Clarity and ease dispersed with the winds outside. Not to return for some time, he feared.

Clarity and ease.

A woman with Tahoe-green eyes . . .

Swinging a pair of tanned legs as she sat on a pier . . .

Clarity and ease . . .

CHAPTER SIXTEEN

Children's Hospital, Bethesda, Maryland

The nurse in the radiation unit had grown a thick skin over the years. Seeing sick children, much less their distraught parents, was never easy. One had to steel oneself, take care of business and try not to take any of it home at night. The sight of children's shaved heads, hollow sunken eyes and gaunt frames, the too-familiar look of childlike endurance of impossible and constant pain, were impressions that had to be left at the hospital door. They could not be allowed to intrude into one's personal life. If they did, the nurses and doctors would not be able to function. And finally, might find themselves in a locked ward somewhere for the incurably nervous, possibly insane.

That said, today Nurse Hollister couldn't help noticing a man in her waiting room. From outward appearances, he was a normal thirty-ish white male. Dressed in crisp Oxford blue shirt and chino pants. Expensive running shoes. Ditto his watch, which appeared to be the kind that could go underwater or tell the time for any time zone in the world. The man was not unattractive. Clean shaven, close haircut and piercing blue eyes.

But there was something horribly wrong. Because he was seated, elbows on knees, shoulders hunched over, chewing aggressively on his already torn and bleeding fingers. The man's cuticles were ripped back, and nearly every finger was bleeding. He seemed oblivious to his condition as he continued his unhappy work.

Hollister approached him quietly so as not to upset him. He did not seem to hear her. So, she took a seat at his side. She lowered her voice as one would in talking to a baby. Gently, she reached for one of the man's hands. "Is your child in for treatment?" No response. "You want to come with me for a moment?" Slowly the man rose from his seat in a trance-like state. He docilely followed her into an examining room.

"Here now. Let me help you." As she spoke in soothing tones, Hollister proceeded to wash down the man's bloody fingers. Next, she applied topical cream to his wounds. And carefully placed bandages over the worst. "Here now. Take this cream with you. You might want to keep the bandages on, so you don't do yourself any further damage. Then use this cream. At night, you know what would be good? Place cotton socks over your hands while you sleep. Okay?"

The man nodded. Together, the two returned to the waiting room. He re-took his seat. Nurse Hollister, the woman who never reacted to pain, felt a tear fall down her cheek as she patted the man's shoulder. "There now. Things are going to get better. A lot of kids come through here because we're the best. Our doctors are taking good care of your child. You just gotta take better care of yourself."

With that, Hollister returned to her post. She watched out of the corner of her eye as the man's child was delivered to him from treatment. Noticed as he tenderly took the boy's hand and placed his other hand on the boy's back as they left the clinic.

For the remainder of the day, Hollister forced the experience from her mind. Still, she noticed people's hands for the rest of the day. A glimmer of emotion was trying to break through her well-constructed shell. She fought her feelings. She tried to focus on her husband's new sailboat. On the day's winter sun. On daisies, her favorite flower. On the opera music she so loved. She would be better tomorrow. So, she hoped. As for the man – she rarely had seen such despair and hopelessness. She knew it would be a long journey back to the light for this man.

CHAPTER SEVENTEEN

David worked late into the night preparing Secretary Layton's testimony before the Senate Committee on Environment and Development. He was planning to meet up with him on the Hill.

Instead, he was sidetracked. Way-laid to other duty by the Secretary, with a surprising request.

Layton began by informing him of his new nickname -- 'Dear Boy.'

What the fuck?

"Mrs. Lechman took quite a shine to you in our brief time at her estate. And sadly, I cannot be in two places at once. That is why I thought . . . well was just wondering . . . since you are now 'Dear Boy' and all . . . if you mightn't consent to fill in for me on a personal duty today, and accompany her to the National Press Club for a speech she's to give."

"You mean instead of attending the hearing?" David asked.

"Instead of."

"I don't know what to say," David stammered.

"Just say you'll do it. Personal favor for me. Because you now are 'Dear Boy,'" Layton added with a trace of a smile playing around his mouth.

David didn't know whether to refuse or laugh. He did neither.

"Of course. If that's what you wish."

Accordingly, the department's driver delivered David to the Middleburg estate by ten. Sybil was dressed in an expensive lavender suit. Her only nod to mourning was a large black silk gardenia pinned to her jacket. She carried her little dog, a Yorkshire Terrier named "Pushkin," around whose neck was tied a black grosgrain ribbon, in keeping with the occasion. Her expensive jasmine perfume preceded her into the back seat of her limousine where David had been directed to wait.

"Hello, my dear. Now this really was not necessary. I told Jeffrey. He has been such a worrier about me. I ask you. I mean, look at me, my dear. I am a wealthy widow. Not a problem in the world. It is how one deals with life, always remember that . . ."

She prattled on as the car made its way down her long drive heading for Washington thirty miles away.

"Think of poor Rose Kennedy, all the worries that poor woman had. As she was fond of saying – 'It is not what happens to one in life that matters but how one deals with it' . . . You seem like someone who knows that . . . Oh, do not answer, I can tell."

"Here now, what am I thinking? There are fresh Bloody Mary's in the cabinet here. Cook prepared them for our little trip . . ."

Perhaps they were soul mates after all. Because nothing suited David more right now than the thought of an ice-cold Bloody Mary, loaded with vodka, a fresh stem of celery waving above the rim of the glass.

"God bless cook," David thought.

'Dear Boy' was along for the ride, more willingly now, thanks to cook's thoughtfulness. There were 'stops' before the Press Club, he learned in due course. First, a mortician in McLean, Virginia. "Just on the way, my dear," Sybil had assured him. He was to wait in the car while she selected the color of satine lining to Horace's casket. From the car window, David glimpsed a pasty-face mortician delivering Sybil to and from the car.

He made a mental note – when he died, no morticians. "I'd better write that down somewhere," he thought. But where? In his will? Should he see a lawyer? Life was just getting better . . . and once again she was in her seat, pouring them their second loaded drink. Well, she would get no arguments from him!

Next, the car turned north on the Beltway to a newly completed building on Wisconsin Avenue behind the Saks Fifth Avenue store. Sybil explained she needed to drop off a list of guests for a store opening she was heading.

"There is this new special events person," she explained. "No sense of politics. None. The opening is to benefit the Lechman Trust for Childhood Cancers . . . everyone in town will be coming . . . by the way, remind me to get you your invitation, you simply must attend . . . do you have a girlfriend? Silly question, of course you must. She is invited as well of course. Do not worry yourself about donations, I understand your position. You will be my guests. Least I can do for your trouble with me today. Besides, my guess is it will do you good to have a luxurious night out . . ."

"Our friend, the President will be there of course, such a lovely man . . . except, my dear, when it comes to grief. The man has been positively cloying about Horace. I simply cannot stand one more person's sympathy . . . ah, here we are, I won't be a moment . . ."

With that, once again the Widow jumped from the limousine, her little dog still clutched in her arms. A store security guard made an attempt to waylay her at the store's double doors. From the window he had cracked open, David could hear her response as she breezed by him,

"Fiddle dee dee!"

Soon enough, she was back in the car offering him a third drink. David refused, and Sybil waved him off.

"No? Speak for yourself, young man. When I have to speak in public, I require fortification!"

With that, the woman downed another on their way to the Press Club.

The National Press Club, one would imagine, is an elegant conclave attended by the nation's media elite, where big thoughts are addressed. In actuality, it takes up one floor of an aging building in downtown Washington. As one exits the elevator, there is a large membership desk such as one might see in an older hotel. Beyond the desk are coatrooms, restrooms, a restaurant, and a number of meeting rooms of various sizes.

It is not smoke-filled.

It is not special.

Except, perhaps, in one's imagination.

Sybil Lechman, Chairman of the Lechman Children's Cancer
Research Trust, had been invited to speak long before her husband's
death. As the "Widow," Sybil already had attended a contentious
meeting with the trust's medical board. Only two days after the
accident on the Bay, she had attended their quarterly meeting, stunning
everyone in attendance, who assumed she would be at home, mourning
her loss. Her no-nonsense demeanor, despite the lavender suit and
strange little dog, soon dispelled any such misconceptions.

Accordingly, the meeting was called to order and oncology
doctors provided their latest list of applicants to receive costly, leading
edge cancer therapy. They briefed board members on the comparative
receptivity of each applicant, the theory being that the stronger
applicants would make better candidates for the rare, still experimental
treatments.

Much of the trust's work followed early research referred to in
the medical literature as "Magic Bullet" treatment. A patient's own
blood was drawn and chemically bonded with radioisotopes. The
altered blood was then re-injected back into the patient to search out

and kill cancerous cells, leaving healthy cells alone. Horace Lechman, an early believer in the therapy, had founded the trust to make this expensive, but promising treatment available to children with limited resources.

As it happened, there were fifteen applicants for their current consideration, and just five slots available. Briefing packets were passed out containing brief biographies and medical histories of applicants as well as financial histories of their parents or guardians.

Before the chief physician began his usual briefing, he attempted to make a flowery speech about their late benefactor.

But Sybil would have none of it.

"No, thank you, but no. Not today. Now then, when might we meet these children and their parents?"

The board members and doctors, stunned by her unusual request, took a few moments to react. During the three years of the trust's existence, they had carefully adhered to a system of patient/board apartheid, never meeting candidates or sponsors. The system allowed the board's attention to remain focused on facts, while never fully engaging members' emotions to the potentially life or death decisions before them. Sybil's request would breach that all-important safe-guard, bringing them face to face with potential recipients.

The doctor was the first to recover.

"Mrs. Lechman, I believe I can speak for the entire committee when I say how truly impressed we are to have you here today under such trying circumstances. Do you suppose you might want us to reschedule these matters for a better time? I am certain everyone would understand if . . ."

Sybil erupted.

"Better time?! As we all sit here in the bloom of good health. What possible better time? No, I insist that we keep to our schedule. Now then. When may we meet these individuals? Oh yes, I can see from your reactions how uncomfortable this might be. How – some – ever . . . my dear Horace insists on results, as you all well know. I shall be reporting back to my husband on our progress and I should not wish to disappoint him . . ."

Reporting back to her husband? Was the woman daft? Her husband was dead. The funeral was to take place later in the week. Obviously, she was still coming to grips with reality. For the time being, however, the widow's reality appeared to consist of returning home after the meeting to inform her husband as to the board's great progress.

But it was her parting words that had them really sitting up straight in their seats.

"By the by. No need to vote today. I wish to announce that the Trust will be treating all applicants. That has been our decision. Horace's and mine. Good day to you all."

But David was unaware of all that, as he accompanied the billionaire's widow to her speaking engagement. He was but the government aide – once again – engaged for service.

"Good afternoon. I'm from the government and I'm here to help you."

As they rode up in the old elevator to the Press Club, David could see Sybil visibly shaking with anticipation. A wave of affection came over him for this brave woman, and he protectively placed an arm around her and whispered, "You'll do a great job," as they exited the elevator. There, reporters merged around her in a wave, shunting David to the rear, which was where he preferred to be anyway.

Watching her approach the podium, David could see that Sybil was determined. Ordinarily, such a presentation would have been minimally attended mainly by medical reporters. Due to her husband's untimely death, however, a tabloid fascination brought them all out. They wanted pictures of the grieving widow. Wanted to catch ahold of the story of the week. Never mind childhood cancer cures. Those could wait awhile longer.

David noted Sybil's shaking hand as she took a sip of water before speaking. Several flash bulbs popped in her direction, taking her further off balance, but she quickly recovered her composure. Then, in laudable high style, Sybil delivered an informative and heart-felt summation of the magic bullet therapy and the trust's substantial success rate.

As she spoke, audience members appeared to be taken with the 110-pound woman in lavender suit. Her determination and commitment seemed to run roughshod over their prurient interests concerning the size of her new fortune, at least temporarily.

One member of the audience in particular caught David's attention. Seated near the back, the man did not resemble a reporter, being casually dressed. He had red hair and his piercing eyes remained glued to Sybil while she spoke. Without looking down he distractedly picked at several fraying white bandages that oddly covered his fingertips. Bits of the protective gauze had fallen onto the table in front of him.

Proving to David, once again, that Washington was filled with real people dealing with real problems. Stereotypes of the nation's capital always left that part out. It was reality and dailiness that so often escaped national attention. These were his thoughts as he watched the man watch Sybil.

After the event, Sybil's car picked them up at the entrance. She had said not a word during the leave-taking. As the car headed towards Washington's West End to drop David at his building, Sybil carefully placed Pushkin in a basket between them. Turning her attention to him, her gaze was steely. For the first time, David noticed the woman's eyes. They were grey. And just now, they seemed the grey of a winter's storm.

"Now see here, David. I feel I must ask you a serious question. What exactly has Jeffrey been up to lately with my husband?"

David was stunned at her abruptness, at the subject matter. What could she be driving at?

She continued.

"Yes, yes, I understand you are Jeffrey's man. And knowing Jeffrey as I do – for many years, I might add, – I know he would not have anyone on his personal staff but someone of impeccable loyalty. How-some-ever, my husband is now dead, or so they tell me. And I really am less than satisfied with it all. Now then, what can you tell me?"

Sybil looked at him expectantly. She seemed pleased with herself, having boxed him in on all counts. She had given him permission to break trust. To share secrets. Trouble was, he knew too little. As an arresting officer might observe, "We don't have enough to hold him."

He knew furniture had been thrown about in the Oval by the most powerful man on earth. He knew that Jeffrey had a volatile relationship with the Commander in Chief. He recalled a conversation in the spa by someone who mistook him for Horace Lechman. He knew some sort of payment was involved. He knew he had dodged bullets most probably meant for her husband. But, as Max had said earlier, "So what?"

"Look, I know you must be aware that I am rather low on the totem pole. Secretary Layton is the President's personal appointee. I know he regards both you and your husband as very dear friends. I am nothing more than a bird sitting on the window ledge outside looking in."

Sybil seized on that. "Exactly. That is my point. Outsiders often see things they are not meant to see. Have perspectives that are different. That is all I am asking here. From that ledge, my dear, what did you see?" Sybil waited again, expectantly. He had to come up with something. She needed something from him. From anyone. He was the closest. It was his turn to help the Widow deal.

He chose his words carefully. "I suppose you are aware of your husband's interest in natural resource sustenance. As well, you may be aware of Matthew Walker's program to merge our interest in resource restoration with international development. It's a new way of looking at natural resources – kind of a mix of State Department goals with environmental and strategic goals. Horace seemed four- square behind the idea . . ."

The storm grey eyes homed in on him. "Go on."

" . . . and so, this Northern Japan trip . . . he was providing private funds to work with Japan's Ainu Indians in creating a destination hot springs resort . . .I myself, have not been brought in on any other aspects . . . if indeed there are other aspects. . . . So, you see, I am afraid from my perch, I have really not observed all that much. I wish that I could offer more . . . but I . . . just . . . cannot." There. He had got through it. Would it be enough? He doubted it.

Her anger surprised him. "Well, then. Young man! I strongly suggest that you investigate. Because there is far more going on here than meets the eye. I am convinced of it. I shall not divulge personal details to you except to tell you I believe something was – is – afoot. Matthew is up to something. My husband was a party to it. Jeffrey knows. Jeffrey knows. For the time being, you say you do not know. How long will such ignorance last? I wonder. You have a wife and two children, I understand."

David was shocked at her knowledge of him. One minute she was talking about his having a girlfriend, the next moment, the scales had come off, and she showed a thorough knowledge of him. He would not discount the Widow again. She was one smart woman.

She continued, ominously: "Fly too high my dear, and the weather can be deadly."

The car pulled up to the curb. The driver had gotten out and was now holding the passenger door open for David. He didn't know what to say . . . "Mrs. Lechman . . ."

"Sybil . . ."

"Sybil . . ."

She reached for his hand, pressing it between her two hands. Again, with the eyes. "Thank you, dear boy. I shall be looking out for you. But remember, as you are on that ledge, keep your eyes open. My Jeffrey is a good man. You will be just fine."

With those words, David found himself standing on the curb, watching the taillights of the shiny car drive away. What the hell? "Fine," she said?

Why the hell wouldn't he be fine?

Ledge? What ledge? Was he a big fat politician? A person privy to Presidential secrets? Or was he a person who was just going to work every day for a decent paycheck to support his wonderful sons? So, he could buy that liveaboard in Seattle . . . Wasn't he just. . . what? . . . fiddle-dee-dee.

CHAPTER EIGHTEEN

Washington, to those who reside there, is a small town. Not a big city, as some would have you believe. Around every corner, down every shopping aisle, are friends, colleagues, casual acquaintances –all refugees to the government enclave, all with their own 'back stories.'

In David's village on the Potomac, so-called 'power center of the world,' a lawyer turned lobbyist like David Kelly can find himself mingling with cabinet members, White House officials, billionaires, billionaires' crazy wives, reporters, even the occasional assassin. At one time or another, they all show up. Can be, at any given time, in the same room.

Village lore covers such odd couplings: "Politics makes for strange bedfellows."

Here, issues and beliefs are determined by one's role in the village. 'Where you stand depends on where you sit.' The electorate wonders where idealism went. For David, the answer was easy: Lost in the pragmatism of village mores.

And yet, as he well knew, it was pragmatism that kept things moving along. If idealistic laws were the ends, 'pragmatism,' (in the form of conciliation, filibuster, line-item veto, splitting the baby down the middle, redefining 'baby' to mean another dam on the Sacramento River), was the means. Some refer to Capitol Hill as a sausage factory. And in that factory, David viewed himself as a wholly competent 'cook.' Nothing more.

Until now.

Now, he found himself caught between a personal mid-life crisis and the nutty ramblings of a very rich woman in lavender.

As his circumstances mixed together in a jumble of incoherent and paranoid thoughts, his own unravelling was becoming an increasing possibility. Consider the evidence, he argued with himself. Two friends had nailed him on it. He talked to exotic salt-water fish. He was drinking more than usual. . . fiddle-dee-dee . . .

. . . .he had a date with a more than acceptable blond soap opera TV actress, yet followed women with auburn braids around town, like some two-bit stalker. He was torn with guilt about his sons, wanting to turn back the clock to 'Julie time.'

"Ernie Fields, his ass."

He bought himself a new lightweight kayak for Potomac forays – hoping that would help. It didn't.

Today, as he descended the majestic steps of the United States Capitol, flanked by military guards and anti-terrorism Jersey barriers, he thrust his hands into the pockets of his raincoat. Something odd. Not his coat. He must have grabbed someone else's after the meeting.

Whose, then?

A piece of paper was tucked in an interior pocket. As he unfolded it, he knew. Layton. A black circle, red star logo on the correspondence meant he would not be returning the coat before reading the note. For this criminal turn of mind, he had Sybil Lechman to thank.

He searched the sidewalk between the Capital and the Supreme Court for a neutral location in which to read the contraband material, say, an empty park bench. But with security being what it was these days, there were prying eyes everywhere. Funny how one only noticed that fact when one had something to hide. Men on roofs in combat fatigues aiming high-definition rifles at people as they passed through official Washington's doors? No problem. Unless one were carrying a bomb, a firearm, or as today, someone else's private correspondence. A cabinet secretary's, at that.

Home was David's best bet. Once he was safely inside his apartment he latched the door. Still standing in his foyer, he read the note. The message was directed to Layton personally, handwritten on UniStar stationary.

"UniStar wishes to report a recent diplomatic message from China to Japan which we have intercepted: It appears that our work activities have been noticed. China has warned Japan and is demanding deep and immediate inspections of all nuclear sites in Japan to assess Japan's program."

What the hell? Japan was not a militaristic nation. The UniStar note continued:

"Our work, as you know, heretofore has been known to be peaceful. We need you to be aware of China's concerns, as stated in their communique. Also, UniStar can report that as a result of our program, Japan possesses 85 tons of the uranium hexafluoride (UF6) gas."

The note concluded.

"Please advise ASAP. Due the delicate balance of defense options in the Asian theatre, our company wishes further instructions before proceeding further."

David's knowledge of nuclear energy was limited. He struggled to recall. Wasn't uranium enriched so that it could be used as fuel in nuclear reactors? And didn't further enrichment create atomic weapons? Holy shit. Sybil was right. What was Layton up to?

Worse, why had he read the stupid note? It was none of his damned business. Who died and made him James Bond? Better not to know. Always better not to know. Bird on the ledge: take care. What had the widow warned? Better not to fly too high, the weather can be deadly.

At a basement listening post a few blocks from the White House, David Kelly's phone was ringing. Still standing in Layton's open raincoat in his hall, David jumped at the noise. As he answered – again the click and pause -- a tape began recording. Key words would trigger analysis of the conversation later. If certain words were not spoken, the tape likely would sit dormant alongside other tapes in his file.

David answered on the first ring. It was Monica, calling again from New York. Wanting to know what to wear for their "date." David knew this was a mistake. But loneliness countered his better judgement. To have someone in the world who wants to call, never mind what's said once the conversation begins. Just to be having a conversation, any conversation, for a while would have to be enough. It had been so long since Julie had cared to talk, David was starting to doubt that anyone would ever again. Care to talk. With him. About anything.

They chatted amiably for a while. Her excitement at coming to Washington was touching. He told her to dress warmly this time of year. Then rang off. And turned his attention to his wimplefish (Heniochus acuminatus). One had died, and now there were three. Wimplefish did better in groups. So, David set off for Georgetown to see about an adoption at a local aquarium store. And to maybe have an early dinner by himself, to take his mind off things, he thought. He'd check out the bookstore on M Street. It was Wednesday evening.

This was how a legislative "big-wig" spent his evenings. As a normal person. Or so he hoped. He was no spy. Just a man on the ledge. Watching from outside. A simple life for a simple man. Or so he hoped.

"M" Street in Georgetown this winter's eve, after an especially warm day, was a zoo. People took advantage of the unseasonal weather by walking, biking, pushing prams. Too many cars and buses crammed the main intersection at Wisconsin Avenue. David circled the street, looking for parking. Suddenly, just ahead of him, a car pulled out. He began turning into the space, but traveling from the opposite direction, a late model Mercedes convertible with the top down, made a U-turn in the middle of the street, and claimed his space.

"Hey asshole!"

David wanted to stop and claim his space from the Mercedes, but traffic already was backing up behind him. As he passed the car, he noticed an attractive young woman seated in the car's passenger seat, a woman with an auburn braid to there.

'Dream Girl!' He no longer gave a damn about some lost parking space. Instead, his mind wandered off. To the real thing. Not some soap opera actress from New York. But an athletic woman, her tanned legs showing beneath a crisp white tennis skirt. Perfection. As he continued his evening, he found himself looking for the woman in the crowds. At the bookstore. At dinner. In the aquarium store.

On the way home, he told his new Wimplefish about her. About their life in Seattle. About how great it would be. He saw nothing strange in this. His fish often heard his stories. They were peaceful creatures. Swimming along silently. Completely comfortable in their environment. Like he wanted to be. Someday.

CHAPTER NINETEEN

Falls Church, Virginia

Where do assassins live? This one lived in a neat white two-story colonial brick in Falls Church, Virginia. With hunter green shutters and trim. He had a wife and two children. Both boys. The children attended Sunday School. They were home schooled. Television viewing privileges were restricted. The family had a computer, but it was located in the living room, in full sight of adults, and was equipped with a parental lock.

How much money do assassins make? One could say they earn roughly in the pay range of governmental Senior Executive Service personnel.

Why do assassins . . . you know . . . assassinate people? Most, like this one in Virginia, grew into the job. "Killing 101" was taught recruits in the Marine Corps. Standard stuff. Honors for excellence in combat meant the opportunity to take further training as a Navy Seal, the crème de la crème of paramilitary professionals.

This assassin was growing older. With a family to support, he signed up with the Special Forces mainly for the extra pay stipends. He also had grown to love mucking about in jungles searching out and killing bad guys. And he was good at it.

One particular assignment did trouble him, however. The assignment was to take out a local Mexican drug dealer, a middleman. Like himself, this criminal was in his line of work to support his family. And the family was relaxing together on a Sunday afternoon. That is when the men broke down the man's front door, walked past his wife and children standing in the hallway, and machine-gunned the man as he was seated in his living room reading the newspaper. The men retraced their steps, back past the wife and horrified children, and out the front door. The assassin had seen death many times in his career. Most of those times, he had caused it. But the look on those children's faces stayed with him. They would visit him at night. When he tried for the relief of sleep.

After a number of years, he was rotated back Stateside, his record nearly perfect. Leon Barshevsky and his comrades needed a stable of such men. Men they could count on for results. For special assignments. It was particularly helpful that the man had a family. That was a connection that could ultimately be used to engender loyalty and silence. In short, this particular assassin, Frank, to his friends, was blackmailable. An added positive quality in this line of work. And so, extra money was dangled. On top of his top pay rate would come bonuses paid for each special assignment.

The assassin, Frank, to his friends, signed both of his children up at the exclusive Madeira School, a school attended mostly by children of diplomats, government officials, and the media elite. It was the notorious school whose head mistress years earlier had gunned down her diet doctor lover, Dr. Herman Tarnower. But that brief smudge on the school's extraordinary vitae had long since been forgotten.

Today, as ever, Madeira was ivy covered, offering its lucky students, soccer, polo and crewing on the river nearby. Children were assigned their own horses at the stables. English riding was a requirement. Ninety-eight percent of Madeira School graduates went on to higher education. In short, the excellent schooling prepared students for lives of security, success and privilege. Would the assassin, Frank, to his friends, take on the assignments needed to give this to his children? In a heartbeat.

As assignments increased in difficulty, the assassin, Frank to his friends, was already fully committed financially. But things grew far more complicated when his younger son fell ill with an especially virulent form of childhood cancer. The family's generous medical plan carried most of the expenses. For the rest, the assassin, Frank to his friends, picked up odd jobs on the side. It became known within his elite 'community' that for him, no job was too small nor too large. He received his orders from a tree trunk along the river banks. He checked the tree according to a predetermined schedule.

His next assignment would be difficult. Now they wanted him to take out a South American drug capo. He was to go alone to the man's fortress-like home. Carrying no identification. If he were caught or killed, he knew it would be his problem. America would never claim the body. Funds were placed in an escrow account for his wife to access in any event. Either way, if he returned or not, the funds still would be there. For his family, it was a "win-win." For him personally, more problematic. But Frank saw his first and most serious role on earth as provider.

The timing of the assignment had no particular meaning for him. In fact, the job would take place during the national mourning period for Horace Lechman. With flags flying at half-staff, Barshevsky wanted no problems. Better to cover all the bases. Send the operatives out of the country on difficult assignments. To be on the safe side. Just to be sure.

The Lechman matter was all but over, save for residual payments for services performed. And the reading of the will. In anticipation of that occasion, Leon Barshevsky already was smacking his lips together beneath his bushy black mustache. So continental, Leon Barshevsky. With his operatives here. And his operatives there.

The President's man. On whom the nation always could count. A man of few words. A man of results.

CHAPTER TWENTY

The Washington Cathedral

David could not recall ever receiving an invitation to a funeral before. But Horace's was a state funeral. Complete with military guard, the world's elite, and oversight by the good ministers of the nation's cathedral. Episcopalianism, it turned out, would be the state religion of choice this day.

There was a light dusting of spring snow on the grounds of the Washington Cathedral – a grand monument to lapsed Catholicism set high on the hill overlooking Georgetown. Next door was the Russian Embassy, set at a slightly higher elevation, the better to aim its radar beams of listening down upon the White House some feet below off in the distance. Were the microwave beams bombarding the cathedral affecting the good ministers' minds? Was anyone checking?

David stood off to the side, taking it all in. Despite the winter's day, the heavy doors of the main church were flung open, flowers were banked inside. A steady stream of black limousines drove up, dispersing world leaders upon God's grace. David wondered what the billionaire would think of it all. Would he appreciate the heartbreak plastered on the face of Matthew Walker? Would he note the stooped shoulders of his president experiencing 'great loss?'

Would Horace be comforted by the President's strong hand, assisting Sybil from the car and up the slick steps of the Church . . . by the presence of Jeffrey Layton following at a respectful distance? David couldn't help but wonder if the three men – Horace, Layton and Walker – shared the horrible secret of a nuclear-armed Japan. Wondered if the three men had played a role in setting up the situation.

And now there were two.

David remembered a quote from somewhere: "Anything awful makes me laugh. I misbehaved once at a funeral." It caught his current mood. For some reason he felt like laughing out loud. In the next breath, he wanted to run down the wide center aisle yelling "Japan has the bomb!" But he didn't do that. Instead, he unbuttoned his wool overcoat and allowed himself to be shown to his seat near the rear, at a distance from those who counted. From the world's leaders. From those who made the rules. From the ceremony and pomp located nearer the front of the vast church. David's view was slightly blocked by a large pillar. That suited him fine. If a hint of a smile should escape his lips, he thought, no one would likely notice.

David noticed a familiar face seated nearby. Nellie Layton. In this official Washington funeral, she too was in her rightful place, taking up the rear. She unselfishly had loaned her husband as official escort to the Widow for the day. Mrs. Layton, being a good politician's wife, knew when to don ceremonial garb, when to furnish tissues or lozenges. More importantly, she knew when to step back, leaving official duties to her husband. After all, she did not bear the will of the people. Her husband was the important one in that regard.

David studied her careful mask of a face. Whereas Julie had renounced the role of 'dutiful Washington wife,' Nellie Layton had taken the other course, selecting the lovely consolation prizes -- exotic vacations, White House dinners, and full shopping privileges. All in all, for this woman of a certain age from Seattle, it was not a bad bargain.

But in the end, would she lose her husband to the Widow? David wondered.

As an organ played the opening filler music, David turned his gaze to Sybil. She had chosen an elegant black hand-tailored Armani suit for the occasion. A lavender scarf peaked from beneath her collar. Unnoted by David or the other attendees was a golden locket at her chest, containing dried lavender and a special message, "Horace loves his lavender lady."

In the end, Sybil had left most of the funeral arrangements to the President and his people. It was not out of indolence so much as her own shrewd judgement that the White House's resources far outweighed her own, and she wanted things to be perfect. They, better than she, knew the correct placement of flags, the required seating for such an estimable crowd, and the security that would embrace them all.

The President had been more like a son to Horace than his own two sons. So, she felt assured the oratory would be warm, and that the room would be filled with men and women whose regard for her husband was of the highest. But there was more. Sybil was feeling her age. She was not sure she could get through such an event, much less plan it. A battle was raging within her over the very nature of this thing they called 'mourning.' Ordinarily, she refused delivery on negative thoughts. Deal with things and move on, that was her motto.

To be sure, she had lost others before Horace. Her parents. A son many years earlier to cancer. Dear friends. Even a husband or two. But none had managed to carve such a crater in her heart as her Horace. None had left her quite so friendless and alone. The payment for such closeness, it seemed, was a grief of unremitting deepness when it was finally wrested away.

And there was another matter, of far more relevance. Her Horace was not dead. He simply had not yet been located on that remote, unused island in the Chesapeake Bay. No phone available. He would still turn up. Her Horace. He was too smart and strong not to. And yet . . .

. . . A funeral in the Washington Cathedral was a hard thing to deny. Surreal. Especially since it was based on a lie. The lie of death. A death that would be denied for some time yet. Sybil kept thinking of how she would describe the day to Horace when she returned home. Then, with a start, she remembered. He would not be at home today. His soul had been entrusted elsewhere. Today was the official transmittal of that parting. Horace would soar above them all this day.

David watched as Sybil gripped the hand railing to steady herself. She appeared to be out of it. Poor woman, he thought. Was there such a woman who would mourn his own passing, he thought again selfishly?

"Ernie Fields, his ass," was his unchurch like thought.

The President approached her, holding her hands in his. Sybil's Horace had the blue eyes of airline pilots. When he looked at you, by God, you were looked at. The President's eyes, on the other hand, were a muted color and they shifted about. One felt an ambivalence and preoccupation with other matters. Maybe, Sybil thought, that's what being a head of state involves. Busy, busy.

Some things David recalled Sybil had said to him that day at the Press Club as she was fighting to overcome her nerves . . .she was a survivor. At the end of the day, Sybil said, the one person on whom she could always count would be herself. She was, after all, 'Sybil.' As her mother often had said, "We do crises well in this family." Her mother passed on the genes. The twin genes of strength and survival. Not to mention the ability to wear hats.

As the official state funeral for the late Horace Lechman began, a famous soprano sang the Battle Hymn of the Republic. The choir followed up. The President intoned. The minister chanted things in Latin. And then, at last, David's commitment was over. He could go home to his fish, his fireplace, his wine, his thoughts.

But Sybil's day was just beginning. Next up was the receiving line. Layton's arm around her waist was the only thing that sustained her during the interminable process. Why must she be nice today? Why must she receive? Because Horace's good friend, the President, had insisted upon it. And for her Horace, certainly not for anyone else, Sybil would measure up on this important day.

Next came a luncheon at the Blair House, across the street from the White House, also arranged by Matthew Walker. The wine, she drank. The chilled salmon got pushed around her plate. She and Jeffrey compared notes. Throughout the morning, one official stood on the sidelines, not venturing into the House of God. He was seen standing in the corridor of the Blair House, sucking on a long, unlit cigar, talking into a cell phone. Leon Barshevsky, as usual, was a disturbing presence, one Sybil could have done without. At one point, Layton whispered in her ear, "I see the Schnauzer is at his post."

At her lawyer's office later that day – why not now, why drag things out? – Sybil was surprised to see Barshevsky again in attendance seated behind Horace's family in the ornate conference room. Besides Leon, Sybil and Layton, the others included wife number three and Horace's six children. Wife number one had died, and number two was currently 'residing' in a substance abuse facility.

The lawyers led off by discussing procedures, then read a remarkably simple, short and clear will, given the fortune involved. Disbursements were as Sybil had been told – Horace had long since provided, and provided well, for everyone in his family. He even funded the rotten apples, in his constant hope they would straighten themselves out at some point. He was not a punitive man. Never had been.

The remaining assets were to go to Sybil. The total amount, she and Jeffrey noted, was considerably less than expected. She was not worried – once one figured in the properties, jewels, pensions, stock options and other assets, Sybil would still be one of the wealthiest widows in America. The surprise was in the substantial sum left to Horace's political party, to the reelection campaign of Matthew Walker, to be precise.

On their way downstairs in the lawyers' private elevator, Layton observed, "Now we know what Barshevsky was doing here. Matt Walker's campaign war chest." For her part, Sybil was relieved the day was drawing to a close. "Politics was always important to Horace. His legacy will live on in Matthew, and in yourself, dear Jeffrey."

Layton's expression steeled as he answered, "Please fair lady. Do not be so hasty as to assign us such credit. There is a talk we must have about all this. Today is not the day."

"Montego Bay. Horace and I were planning on going down there in a few weeks. You must make the trip with me. We can talk then."

As Layton helped Sybil into her car, he accepted. "I shall plan on it. Oh, by the way, one of your lawyers handed me this as we were leaving." Layton gave Sybil a key with a tag attached. "Apparently, there was one remaining safe deposit box, only for your private access.

Up in New York. Now, I am off to the ball and chain. Call me later if you should need anything."

With those words, Layton kissed the lady's hand and gently closed her car door. The sleek limousine slowly edged into traffic. Back to the Middleburg farm. To early blooming dogwoods, bread pudding, closets filled with lavender, and memories. Memories from a decade of marital happiness. A life cut short, time stolen. Unfairness. Injustice. Cold sheets. Tears. Sleepless nights.

On the trip home, Sybil held the key Layton had given her in her palm. When it grew warm, she turned it over. Then she toyed with the string holding the tag. She folded the tag so many times it nearly tore.

At last, she read the tag.

"Lechman Industrial Bank of New York."

Karen Hagestad Cacy

CHAPTER TWENTY-ONE

Tags and papers. Some held more importance than others. Some fairly reeked of significance. Of life changing potential. David Kelly was fingering his own document this evening. One with a round black circle and red star logo in the corner. The note he had found posited inside Layton's raincoat. What to do? Destroy it? Fool! It was a message of high confidentiality directed to the President's eyes only!

Not for him, a bird on the ledge.

A message that would change geopolitics in the Far East for years to come.

In David's mind, he already knew enough. From the ledge. For instance: He began his lifelong career in public service as an attorney for a Pacific Northwest-based environmental group. They were concerned about over-logging which denuded heavily forested mountains. When spring rains came, rootless soil gave way allowing masses of mud to flow downhill, leaving nothing but ugly patches of cut-out slope. Down came whole hillsides. Into streams and rivers below. Fouling drinking water for domestic stock and wildlife alike. David's ethic had always been in favor of the environment. Its preservation. Its sustainability. His comfort level in being on that side was immense. He enjoyed the face he saw staring back in the mirror each day.

And now? Lately, things had grown much more complicated. Somehow, he had morphed from a corduroy- slacks wearing eco-warrior into a strategic, geopolitical legislative minion. In just a few short years, it seemed, the world had changed, taking his footing from under him. The era of resource wars was quickly approaching. A combination of global climate changes and dwindling natural resources were forever altering the direction of American foreign policy.

With global conflicts already underway for oil, water, and other valuable resources, the growing trend in strategic circles was to place resources at the center of military debates. Somehow ideology and politics now took a back seat to the Pentagon's check list of who had what, when will we need it, and how can we go get it? David, by his work on the President's Wilderness Legislation unwittingly fell in the center of this roiling vat of political pragmatism.

At some point, his environmental legislative work had passed from idealistic to cynical. His tactics were the same. It was the mission that had changed. Had slipped from his grasp. Now, he had had enough.

Today, he wanted to cast the letter into his fireplace. Be done with it. But then, he also wanted to open a small restaurant somewhere at the beach. People wanted to do a lot of things they never did.

He knew he needed to understand more about UniStar. Had Layton made the deal that gave Japan nuclear secrets? Well, had he? Was Layton more like 'Godfather,' than benign cabinet member? How would he explain the shift to David? "Don't worry, my son. It's not personal, it's only business."

When in hell had their work crossed the line to 'it's only business?' Where was David that day? And what other nefarious schemes might be contained in the man's briefcase? How many lies was he telling David in the course of their work?

Flying high was for others.

He had no need to know other's business. But as soon as that thought came into his mind, he caught himself in a lie. He was curious. Always wanting to know. Wanting to be included in the action. A man doesn't make it to the cabinet level by sitting back, taking things as they come. David knew who he was. He just hated having to admit it.

How else could one explain his failure to cast the letter into his fireplace in the first place? His obsession with UniStar? Why did he care two cents about their secrets? About Japan having the nuclear bomb? So, what? So, fucking what?

He switched on the Sunday morning talk shows. Today's subjects seemed to be partisan politics, about the President's approval ratings which, by the way, were just fine. "Good for you," David muttered. "Good for all of us." He decided the chilly day called for an order of his homemade Indian curry, and an end to thinking about things he could not change.

He enjoyed his meal along with a bottle of German beer beside his fireplace. Later, snow flurries outside, and an excellent new book on exotic saltwater fish momentarily transported him from Washington, and its little intrigues. He had a decent phone conversation with Julie, making plans for the boys' visit during spring break. The thought of seeing them always cheered him.

Soon, he would need to deal with this distance problem. That meant moving back to Seattle. It also meant finding a new job. And integrating back into a social life that by now had been mostly reclaimed by Julie. He had a few friends scattered here and there. But they all knew about the divorce. And he still felt like a jerk. Didn't much want to be reminded that he was a poor husband and father. He already knew that.

The phone rang. He let the machine play out but sprang up when he heard a familiar voice begin recording a message. It was Stan Fisher, his old reporter friend. Stan was with the Associated Press, and he and David went all the way back. Back to the days of their environmental activism. David always enjoyed Stan's calls, filled with local gossip no one else knew.

"Stan. Sorry I didn't pick up sooner. How the hell are you?"

"What, you aren't speaking Japanese yet?"

"What d'ya mean, 'speaking Japanese'"?

"Well, I saw your boss two weeks ago up on the North Island – Hokkaido."

"Nope. Wasn't him. He was in Tokyo though. Sure you didn't see him there?" David's lying was improving.

But Stan was a pro. "Don't spin me, man. I was there. I saw him. Caucasians are hard to miss in the middle of a Japanese hot springs resort."

Jesus. How could he have seen Layton and missed David? Dumb luck, he guessed. One could never overestimate the importance of dumb luck in this life, David thought. He responded, "'Lotta steam in those baths, Stan."

"Hey man. The only steam is what's blowin' outta your mouth. Aw, sure go ahead and deny it. I can check the travel records, you know."

"Tokyo. Like I said. What other nuggets of wisdom have you got today?"

"Another ice cap's ready to break off. This one should take out the West Coast all the way back to Montana."

David was enjoying this. "Isn't it about time for you to try some fly fishing out there then?"

The two continued on awhile as good friends do. Insult upon insult, was the pattern. As well as lame sports analysis. They knew each lied on occasion. The reality of their friendship was that they worked in different, adversarial realms. Territories with slightly different ground rules where the truth was concerned. Yet occasionally, they forgot to remember to lie. Each one could tell by the other's tone and demeanor when such an occasion was taking place.

Their friendship was one of Washington cave dweller communications. But it also was one of two old hands, fencing, jousting, making jokes. Kelly knew Stan would stay on the story. The man was a fucking bird dog. But he had warned him. The media was now tracking Layton's movements. That was the reason for his friend's call. To warn him.

First Sybil. Now Stan. Warnings. Admonitions. Scary problems. On top of his own scary personal life. David opened a particularly excellent bottle of wine. To quell the premonitions. To delay whatever the hell it was that needed delay.

CHAPTER TWENTY-TWO

David stood in the doorway of Secretary Layton's impressive office at the Department of Resource Development. In his hands, he held the Secretary's raincoat. The offending note was tucked neatly in the inside pocket where David had found it. Layton came from behind his desk to take the coat from David. He immediately and silently searched the pocket, extracting the note. His eagle eyes narrowed as he regarded David for an instant, before bellowing for Marge, his secretary.

"Place this in an 'Eyes Only' envelope and personally deliver it immediately to Millie Avignell in the President's office. Any questions?" Marge nodded her understanding.

Layton closed his door behind her.

"Have a seat."

It was not an invitation. This had all the earmarks of one of Layton's infamous 'Come to Jesus' meetings. David didn't care. He had his own issues. He was ready for Layton.

"Bring it on, Mr. Secretary!" he thought.

Ordinarily, when one was in the presence of a cabinet secretary, particularly in the cabinet secretary's own office, one speaks only when spoken to. David broke that code, not believing his own affrontery, as he spoke.

"The contents of that note cannot be news to the President."

"You read it. Might have assumed as much. Not a surprise, you say?"

"No sir. A surprise to myself however. My God, this is our environmental leader, a man who was elected on his promises to support nuclear non-proliferation!"

"He did not begin the Japan adventure . . ."

David stammered, "I . . . I . . . just cannot understand . . . were we a part of this whole deal, with UniStar in Hokkaido? Was Lechman? Are you? Is our wilderness program nothing but a cover for the President's schemes? Have I been lying to Congress? Have you? Has the President?" He could have gone on, but he felt his breath getting short with emotion. He never challenged the Secretary. Didn't happen. Except he just had.

"Are you done?" The Secretary gained back his usual dominance and gravitas. Then he said something peculiar.

"Amy Schwabauer."

David responded, "Sir?"

"I said 'Amy Schwabauer.' Amy was in my second-grade class back in Seattle."

"My God," thought David. "The man is losing his mind."

Layton, attuned to David from years of work, read his face.

"Stay with me. Amy was very frail, white-white skin – a red-head. Wore these thick coke-bottle lens- glasses . . ."

"What the hell?" David thought.

"Every day, Amy came to me after lunch. She gave me, each day for a week, a Dream-sickle. Remember those?"

David did. "Yeh. Orange sherbet coating on a vanilla ice cream bar. Very good."

"Yes, indeed. Excellent. And I was given one several days in a row by our Amy."

David interrupted: "I really am having trouble . . ."

Layton waved him off. "I know, I know. So, anyway, after about a week and a half, Amy came up to me in class. She wanted her money. At first, I didn't understand what in the hell she meant. But she made it very clear. She had purchased a number of Dream-sickles for me, and now she was asking for her payment." Layton waited triumphantly for his story to sink in. David just sat there. He had no idea . . .

"Alright. Let me finish. That, 'Dear Boy,"

David really hated that name.

" . . . That was my first lesson in politics. 'Nothing for nothing.' If you want someone to do something for you, you must have some credit in the old bank account. Get it? Now then, let me bring this back to our current situation.Don't get me wrong, I understand your position. Maybe I have been less than honest with you. You have been doing a yeoman's job on the Hill based on your own beliefs. The environment. Sustainability. Being on the side of truth and justice. Am I right? Am I right?"

He didn't wait for an answer. "David. David. Our country is not the same entity it was when we both started. Countries anymore are nothing more than giant corporations, give or take . . ."

David could not stand the cynicism. "I'd have to disagree with you. We have a Constitution, a Bill of Rights. A voting system. Not this cynicism."

Layton continued.

"A quiet revolution based on necessity has, I am afraid, already superseded our laws on the books. We are bartering for our very lives, based on dwindling resources. We must indebt countries having scarce resources we know we will need on the front end, so that we will be able to come in on the back end and collect. Get it?"

David could not believe what he answered. From somewhere deep inside him, a long wail of grief made its way out. "I'm out. I quit."

Layton responded.

"I'm not surprised you'd say that. However, I do not accept your resignation. Let me make you a counteroffer."

David could no longer feel his legs. What had he just done? Resigned? And now a 'counter-offer' was coming?

"First off. Goes without saying, not a word about this UniStar business. I know you will abide by that. Next, help me out for another six months on this legislation. Now that you see the practicality of it, you cannot forget the original intent of saving miles and miles more of the world's wilderness areas has to be a good thing."

He looked at David for some sign he had heard his words. David was staring straight ahead.

"And there is another matter. Sybil Lechman."

Sybil Lechman? What about Sybil Lechman? What did she have to do with this?

"Between me and you, I love her. We have been close for years, during many of our marriages. Now she is alone. I will be alone soon. Oh, don't look so surprised. Nellie and I have been in mutual détente for years now. Sybil has taken a shine to you. She needs someone by her side as she goes through the next few weeks. Someone she trusts. That could very well be you. I would forever be in your debt!"

Now David's arms went numb. What was going on here?!

"I have a quid pro quo for all this . . ."

Shit. He didn't want to be here. Quid pro quo?

"You and I will be getting out soon. I know you want to return to Seattle. I have friends. You know that. A political job out there will be no problem. Think of this as your golden parachute. So, do we have an understanding? Will you do this for me? One last personal favor?"

David's head nodded mechanically up and down. His legs somehow supported his body as he rose from his seat and made his way back to his office.

Layton took his behavior as a "Yes."

Both took it as a "Yes."

What a truly strange day for them both.

CHAPTER TWENTY-THREE

'Dear Boy' fastened his seat belt in preparation for take-off. The Widow took no such precaution. She was on her feet, pouring champagne cocktails for herself and David as the well-appointed Lechman corporate jet took off over Middleburg fields. Again, as before, David watched the priceless horses, spooked by the plane, take off across the rolling fields, tails flowing gracefully behind them.

As the small corporate jet lifted through a puff of white clouds on this clear day, the well-tended mile-upon-mile of white fencing vouch-saving the security and secrets of the mega-wealthy, quickly faded away.

Sybil had made the usual clucking noises when David had been entrusted to her as 'companion' for her trip to her husband's New York bank. But David, who was developing a true affection and understanding for Sybil, could read her relief. Truth be told, he rather enjoyed the break from serious matters.

Sybil had been very kind to him from the beginning under trying circumstances. He noted she had a definite classiness that went a long way to explaining her stature among the important of the world. Coming from a lower background than even her husband, Sybil nevertheless had been a quick study as she rose in society. Whereas

years earlier, her indoctrination into the upper realm might have
appeared forced, now it seemed as second nature. The trick David
could tell, was that there happened to be a real, caring person under the
appurtenances. With Sybil, there was a 'there' there.

And so it came to pass that the two morning drinkers again
found themselves together, and neither seemed to mind. Sybil was not
one to dilly-dally. Several days after the funeral, she already had signed
papers, evaluated properties, re-done her calendar for the year, and
begun the sleep-walking that now was her life.

Boarding the Lechman jet, she already knew all she needed to
know about her Horace. It was these facts she would hold close to her
breast forever. To be sure, there was plenty of unknown territory where
her late husband was concerned. Plenty of secrets. But he was an
honorable man, and that was enough for Sybil. She had felt no
particular interest in knowing his secrets, so long as he had kept on
loving her and holding her hand beneath the covers at night.

In New York, with 'Dear Boy' in tow, Sybil entered the bank,
and the two were instantly whisked upstairs by the bank president.
What a difference large amounts of money could make, David thought.
When he went to his bank, he stood in a line with the rest of the rabble.
Periodic disagreements? The bank always prevailed. With that famous
simpering customer service smile as they cut one's legs off.

"It's nothing personal, sir. It's only business."

The bank president's flourishes of extreme service to The Widow included hot tea served in fine china cups. David watched her as closely as geologists watched Mt. St. Helens, for the building steam vent that would result in a mega-ton blast. He smiled to himself as he nearly felt sorry for the obsequious president, a man who knew neither when to stop, nor what the risks were of continuing.

But continue, he did. The condolences. The expectation of her own sorrow. Finally, predictably, Sybil put her foot down and demanded to be shown to the safe deposit box, there to be left alone. David walked with them to the perimeter as the bank's chambers unfolded like layers of an onion. He thought these vaults were perfect receptacles to hold people's secrets.

Sybil made the final steps alone, key in hand. Key and master key fit perfectly, and now, she was alone . . . ready for . . . what exactly? She had no idea. Jewels? Bonds? Cash? Deeds? Promissory notes? Inside was a single white envelope addressed to her.

"My Turtle Dove."

David could see her react through the glass wall. She nervously glanced up at a security camera recording her movements. She would have none of that. Abruptly, she fled to the outer vault, grabbing David's arm as her speeding high heels clicked against the bank's marble floor. The president followed at a distance, having finally understood this was one widow not to tangle with. David caught a glimpse of the hapless executive on their way by. Was that relief on his face? Probably.

Inside the car on their way back to the airport, she held the unopened letter tight. As the car pulled onto the tarmac, she carefully folded the letter and placed it inside of her blouse. And they stepped from the car. Boarded the plane, two passengers on their way back to Middleburg, Virginia.

Inside, the pilots went about the business of flying. The passengers were served martinis by the attendant, and David watched as Sybil retired to her private cabin. He heard a click as she locked the door from the inside. It was a smooth flight, and David was pleased to receive the martini chasers and wonderful lunch. With Sybil tucked away, he could think of his own life. Of papers bearing secrets. Of the wife gone by. Of two adorable boys. What had Layton promised? Six months. Ah! Time enough to divest his holdings in Washington. Time enough to negotiate for that liveaboard. Time enough, he hoped to locate Dream Girl.

Inside her cabin, Sybil secured the door and plumped the pillows on the bed. Before lying down, she positioned a photograph of Horace on the nightstand within her gaze. Then, after a long sip of her drink, she removed the letter from her blouse. She carefully opened the sealed envelope. There, in Horace's excellent ink penmanship, was what he wanted her to know. From the grave.

Suddenly, the plane dropped several hundred feet. The pilot came on the intercom nearly immediately. "Sorry about that, Mrs. Lechman. Bit of a wake from the plane in front. Shouldn't happen again." Sybil, a seasoned flyer, scarcely heard the apology. She already was engrossed in Horace's message. It was long. Ten pages in all. When she had read it, she re-read it. Then she began in the middle and read selected passages. She turned to the end, reading the final paragraph. She folded it and replaced it in its envelope. She finished her drink and called for another. Then she reopened the letter and read it again. Finally, the letter was returned to its rightful place at her breast.

Sybil, warmed by the liquor, took a little nap. Horace was with her. They made love and at the very end, his leg stiffened in one of the cramps he used to get. He looked so ridiculous, hopping around the cabin on one foot, his face contorted in pain. Sybil crawled after him and reached up to massage the injured leg muscle.

"Turtle dove. Yes. You take such good care of me. In every way."

The two finished the plane trip on the floor. Sybil pulled her mink coat off the bed and on top of them. They were warm. They were together. The leg relaxed. Soon, Horace was sleeping soundly in Sybil's protective arms. What was it about this man, she thought? Who would see him like this? Who would believe what a companion he was?

The pilot's voice over the intercom wakened Sybil as the plane began its final descent onto the Mellon private jet strip in Marshall, Virginia. "Mrs. Lechman, we should be on the ground in about fifteen minutes." Sybil wondered what she was doing on the floor, with her coat draped across her. Then the crinkle of paper against her chest reminded her. There was no Horace. There were no leg cramps. Only secrets. Entrusted to the widow.

The car would drop Sybil and then take David to his home. David was curious about the letter. He rather expected Sybil to say something on the ride back. Nothing. He got nothing. She kissed him on the cheek as she was helped from the car. The car began its roll down the long drive. Then stopped. Backed up. Sybil had a last word. His window was unrolled by the driver. Sybil leaned in.

"I must not say too much. You understand. However, you may tell the Secretary that it is a new day. Horace knew. Horace knew. And now so do I. And soon the world will also."

Then, she leaned back. The car window was re-closed. And the big black car made its way once again down the drive.

"Too damned many secrets," thought David. At the same time, he was thrilled to be in on things. To be on the inside near interesting people. 'Dear Boy' was having himself quite the ride these remaining months in Washington.

What is it they say?

A little knowledge can be a dangerous thing?

How about a whole shit-load?

CHAPTER TWENTY-FOUR

Seattle, Washington

The bulk cargo vessel bearing the Japanese name "Maru," was escorted into a private terminal at the Port of Seattle. The ship was carrying Pacific Northwest timber that had been farmed in Oregon, shipped to Hokkaido for milling, and now was being returned stateside for final sale. The ship was heavy in the water, and the customs officer was too busy today to check all the load. Or so he said.

Behind the massive stacks of wood being off-loaded were two smaller shipping containers strapped down out of sight. Each bore the distinctive UniStar logo. A United States Park Service semi backed into position at the dock to receive the containers. Quickly, by forklift, they were loaded onto the truck. The driver stood at a distance from the rear of the truck with a remote control in his hands. Once the containers were loaded, he mechanically closed a heavy leaded interior door. Then the outer truck door.

The driver negotiated the big truck through the Port's security gates – U.S. Park Service trucks were never stopped – and into downtown Seattle traffic. From there, he headed up country via

Interstate 80, east bound. The Northwest rain washed his truck clean as he headed up into the still snowy Cascades.

Considerably South of Seattle

Much farther south in the hemisphere, a second ship was docking. The man riding onboard this aged freighter had wanted to arrive at his South American destination without the benefit of immigration formalities. Fair to say, his mission would not be welcomed in all quarters of the country. At home, his wife and family waited for him to do his job quickly and return safely.

The first thing he noticed was the humidity that had been building as the ship approached the shoreline. It reminded him of his days in the Special Forces when the jungles swallowed up scores of men with guns. Leaving the ship, he walked into town and checked into a small hotel that had the habit of not asking questions. For this service, they were paid handsomely. Far more than such a shabby little room ordinarily would bring.

After dinner, the man began his research. He already knew that his important subject on occasion slipped free of his security detail to visit a certain lady in a rough part of town. From this lady, he received special favors. Ones he could not receive anywhere else. For these unique services, he was willing to take the risk. A man, after all, was a man. And the man's machismo, fed by cocaine, would once a month overrule his customary cautiousness.

A killer needed to know his prey. Their vulnerabilities. Where the point of contact could be made. If one were willing to make the effort, research would reveal about the most careful and regular of souls some irregularities in their lives. It was these irregularities the killer would exploit. The ultimate price this man would pay for being all too human, it turned out, would be death.

The details of the kill were fairly simple. Timing. Pay-offs. A quiet gun placed just so. The perfect escape into the jungle with a few well selected amigos. The killer would be back with his nice family in Arlington, Virginia in no time at all. And would wash out the hair dye that had concealed his normally red hair.

Karen Hagestad Cacy

CHAPTER TWENTY-FIVE

Washington, to those who reside there, is a small town. Not a city by any means. For around every corner, down every shopping aisle, are friends, colleagues, and other United States refugees to the government enclave. The smallest percentage of these are elected officials. Most come to town without benefit of a vote of "the people."

Bureaucrats like David Kelly commonly are vilified when political decisions go south, even though they are unaccountable to voters. Viewed as 'government functionaries,' who would slam a window on a person's fingers promptly at 4:59 p.m., closing time at the local post office, they are thought to be people sitting in safe municipal jobs. Dunderheads. Who would give them a thought?

As David put together Walker's Wilderness Bill, he worked with agency lawyers, analysts, and others. Now in the briefing stage, he was on the Hill visiting young staffers whose influence could make or break their chances. Many whom David briefed were fresh out of college, and it was their impressions he needed to nail down. Because with members' increasingly out-of-control workloads and campaign commitments, it was the young staffers on whom elected officials depended for their positions, yay or nay.

The teen carrying coffee in the elevator possibly could be the one standing guard over access to an important member. As mother used to say, 'Be nice.' And David was always nice.

Wearing his congenial 'Hill face,' he began his work in the House. He floated Secretary Layton's trial balloon – how might the committee view an aggressive White House plan to reclaim seven-eighths of the Alaskan wilderness? Could the oil companies' cries of anguish be drowned out by the 'Wilderness President's' high-minded plan to save precious resources? Or, as David was coming to believe, would they shut the hell up because they were in on the deal in the first place?

He knew that during the 'end game,' a vote scheduled by the President's party for a Thursday evening would hinge on information on how many opposing members were antsy to fly home for a long weekend. If enough 'no's' blew town early, the vote would be stealthily easy.

The legislative dance was intricate, at times downright comical. One member, he recalled, had not wished to have his vote recorded on a controversial bill. He hid out in the back reaches of his office as the vote was called. The opposition, wishing to force the man's hand, sent Hill guards in search of the errant voter. The guards found the hapless member at the very back part of his office. He was escorted to the floor where he was compelled to vote his conscience.

"It's nothing personal. It's only business."

As he returned to the office, David was satisfied. For a change, Hill staff had seemed buoyed by the vision of the President's plan. An aide of one opposition member had even refrained from delivering his usual rant about the rights of the oil companies. No tantrums. A good sign. David jotted down his notes from the Town Car's back seat. As the big car rounded a corner, a hard object hit him on the leg. It was the Secretary's briefcase that was lodged beneath the seat.

Even as he noted the distinctive gold seal on the flap, David could feel a knot forming in the pit of his stomach. He knew what he would do. Because the post-getting-shot-at David was operating under 'New Rules.' His six-month agreement with Layton was one thing. Knowing was another. What was the sub-strata? What was the deal with Walker and Layton? Would there be another tectonic shift? Would it swallow him up? Or would he be able to calmly leave town, feathers intact? These questions required answers.

As the car entered the department's underground parking structure, David slipped the case under the papers he was carrying. After he was let out, feeling like a common criminal, he made his way to his own car, parked in a dark corner of the garage.

The high-tech black disc located in the center of the floor followed David. It zoomed in on him for a close-up. It noted the license plate of David's car. It performed these tasks noiselessly. Later, the record was there. To assure the government of the inviolability of its facilities.

Once inside, David locked the doors and glanced around to make sure no one was observing his odd behavior. He assumed the cameras were operating. But it was perfectly reasonable for him to make a quick stop at his own vehicle. Perfectly innocent to retrieve something. Or to catch something on the radio. Eat a sandwich. Citizens did all kinds of innocent things in their cars.

It was the middle of a weekday. The building above him hummed with the nation's business. Yet each time someone drove by, David stiffened. 'New Rules' notwithstanding, he was not used to sleuthing.

There was something else to consider: The 'Six Month Pact.' The implied trust. 'Sub-Section Three' no doubt cited there would be no pawing through his boss's private belongings. But 'New Rules' trumped 'Six Month Pact.' His sixth sense told him he was missing parts of the story. Recent events, including the President's outburst, had only heightened his curiosity.

One-way David had been successful in his long career was by being in the know. By being aware of his surroundings, and the moods and actions of those around him. Knowledge was power, affording one the opportunity to take preemptive action. He reminded himself of these reasons as he attempted to justify what he was about to do. Then, with a deep breath, he opened the clasp on the case.

A roll of breath mints rolled out. In a side pocket were five crisp one hundred-dollar bills. A tabloid newspaper was folded to show an article about Leila and Roger Harumi, wealthy supporters of the President. "Another oil baron," he noted. There were department letters. Policy papers. Development reports. His broker's statement.

And . . . hello! What's this? A spreadsheet was folded inside a used commercial plane ticket. The left column was in Kanji script. Across the top, written in English were seven Japanese words. David wrote them down. Under each name was a sum preceded by a symbol for Japanese Yen. At the bottom, amounts were totaled and converted to U.S. currency. The total read "$25.3 million." For what? David wondered.

Sheepishly, David carried the case to Layton's office. His secretary looked relieved to see it. "Oh my God. Thanks. We've been looking all over for this." She grabbed the case from his hands and quickly retrieved the spreadsheet. Then she looked up at him and in a sharp tone asked, "Did you happen to open it?"

"Only to make sure it was Layton's," he lied. But Marge, like Milly Avignell, was no fool. You didn't get to be a top private secretary by misreading people. Her eyes narrowed.

"David Kelly."

"Don't 'David Kelly' me. I know nothing."

"And I believe you. But a word to the wise. Leave well enough alone."

"Marge, what the devil . . .?"

She raised a well-manicured hand in a warning gesture.

"Do not go there. Leave it, okay?!"

With that, Marge, who normally was his ally, his partner in dealing with the 'Grand Pooh-Bah, Himself,' turned her back on him and picked up a ringing phone. Their conversation was over.

David walked out into the corridor more confused than ever.

Seven words . . . $25 million, American . . .then he remembered Layton had another trip to Japan scheduled for later in the month. A trip he had told David would be personal. Like hell, David thought. Like hell!

In his pocket, he felt for the slip of paper.

Bearing seven Japanese words.

Seven words for further study.

Curiosity killed the cat.

Fiddle-dee-dee.

CHAPTER TWENTY-SIX

Seven Words

Later, David did a Google search from his home computer. He carefully entered the words. As he had suspected, they were towns. Located at various locations within the Japanese archipelago. Something else. The news gave him a start. As his saltwater fish swam gracefully along in their little apartment ocean, David re-read the information. Each of the towns shared something in common.

Each location had a nuclear reactor. For peaceful purposes? Of course. For domestic power only. But David knew better. Who else knew? he wondered. Since World War II, he knew U.S. planes regularly searched countries for signs of radioactive debris from nuclear tests. Now, spy satellites performed similar surveillance.

David also knew that times were more perilous than during the Cold War, when only two opponents – U.S. and Russia – faced off. Now, there was a proliferation of nuclear states, operating alongside rogue states and stateless-terrorists intent on joining the elite nuclear club. Technology sharing? Up for grabs. You got the check? We got the information.

Seattle. He mused about his future life there. The life of his darling boys. With nukes trained on them from North Korea . . . China . . . and now . . . Japan.

What had Marge said? "Leave well enough alone."

What had Sybil said? "As the bird on the ledge, keep your eyes open."

He knew he needed to do both.

CHAPTER TWENTY-SEVEN

Washington's Union Station

Sometimes, Jeffrey Layton could be a royal pain in the ass. This was one of those times. He was taking an attitude with David because they were traveling by train instead of flying to New York City. David thought a train ride would do them both good. 'His Highness' disagreed.

Weighed down like a pack animal, David guided Layton to his seat. As they cleared the waiting room, he happened to glimpse a woman's long auburn braid hanging over the back of her wheelchair. He must be cracking up, seeing redheads everywhere he went. Things were getting out of hand. But soon they would be in New York, where Monica would be meeting him. David found himself looking forward to seeing her. Very clearly, he needed a life.

The conductor made final announcements and the train doors clicked shut. The fancy Acela high-speed Amtrak train sped up to its 125-mile per hour cruising speed. The Secretary seemed to relax as he noted the obvious comfort of the special executive coach. The ride was glass-smooth, the seats and appointments first-rate. To further facilitate the thaw, David went to fetch hot coffee.

When he returned, the two rode in quiet for a while. David's thoughts returned to the redhead. He couldn't get her out of his mind. Maybe he should try to locate her. But, how? He had no name. No information whatsoever. His thoughts were interrupted by Layton.

"My, my. You are so deep in thought. Oh, ho! Don't say. Must be that woman you're planning on meeting. An actress, isn't she?"

"Yes. Monica Waters. She's on one of those TV soap operas – 'The Gathering Storm.'

"You bringing her to events?"

"Hadn't planned on it."

"Kelly!" The sharp sound of Layton's voice made several passengers seated nearby look up from their newspapers. "Bring her! That's an order. Pretty woman's always welcome. Besides . . ."

David waited for him to finish.

" . . . besides, we have a tradition to uphold."

"What tradition's that?"

He lowered his voice and leaned in. " . . that fellas in our party can get any woman we want."

David recoiled in disgust. Sometimes Layton could be a real disappointment. This was one of those times. Thankfully, the man dozed off. David was glad of that. He had no further interest in talking.

Monica met him at the station. He had just seen Layton off in a car provided by the mayor. Thank God he would have a day's break from the man. It seemed every time he was directly involved with President Walker, Layton's nervousness rose another notch. And another thing. While he sat back and let David carry their luggage, David noted he kept a weather eye on his own briefcase.

Monica was happy to see David. He had to admit her warmth was a welcome break in his existence. Back at her apartment on West 81st Street, with the redundant door locks and a grand piano taking up most of the living room, the two quickly enjoyed some wine.

Eventually, they found themselves in the bedroom. One- minute Monica was giving him the grand tour, the next . . . well, how long had it been now? Months? Years, even? David knew he was not much of a lover. Too fast. Too selfish. Macho thoughts ran through his mind at first: "He deserved the attention. Didn't he work hard? Hadn't Monica made the first move? Or, had he? Did it really matter who went first?"

Then his mind started playing tricks on him. He wasn't with a beautiful blonde actress in New York. Rather, he felt a liveaboard tip a little as a power boat cruised by. He reached up to touch an auburn braid that had found its way to rest on his chest. He grabbed at the braid, as though it were a lifeline.

"Ow!" Monica's scream of pain brought him out of his reverie, as he quickly withdrew his hand.

"Geez. Monica. I'm sorry. I must have leaned wrong." There he went again, lying was becoming second nature. If 'Story One' is a non-starter, move quickly to 'Story Two.'

And so, it went. The usual things followed. Showers. Dinner out. More wine. Later on, David made his excuses to return to the hotel. "More work to get ready for the news conference with the President." Liar!

Monica had seemed happy despite David's odd lapses, and lame lovemaking. He remembered Layton's demand. "Uh, Monica . . . I wonder if you would be interested in joining me tomorrow . . . for the President's news conference . . . at Gracie Mansion . . ."

Would she?!

"You mean with the President?!"

"That's right. We're announcing some wilderness funding for the state is all. Nothing special. Just a photo opportunity . . . mostly for the cameras . . ."

"Cameras! Then I'll need to pick up my white suit from the cleaners. . ."

Nothing special, indeed. David again observed how the 'civilian world' reacted to experiencing the power of the presidency. In the end, everyone was happy. David did his job, with background briefings to some financial reporters. President Walker was able to collect a few favors as he doled out federal funds. Even Layton appeared pleased for once. Monica wore her white suit and was a striking presence.

In the sea of cameras, and men in dark suits, she stood out like a sparkling jewel. Her tanned skin and perfectly flaxen hair provided the bored reporters with a welcome diversion from Walker's usual soft shoe.

"God bless blondes," the male members of the press corps must have been thinking pretty much in unison. From across the room, David watched as several of them approached her.

"Monica Waters. From 'The Gathering Storm.' My wife watches you every day." One reporter motioned to his cameraman to move in closer for a shot. The cameraman needed no urging as he zoomed in on the B actress.

"Why, yes. That's right. How nice to be recognized."

The second reporter approached, quickly switching off to Monica's character's name. "So, tell us, Annette. What brings you here today?"

"Oh, I'm with David. Kelly. He works for Secretary Layton."

"Layton, you say. Know anything about all that travel he's been doing?"

"Why . . . no, I . . ." Monica struggled to answer.

The reporter continued. "Guess Layton and Walker really haven't been getting along lately. Know anything about that?"

At this, Monica giggled. At least there was a question she could answer. "Oh well. There is something funny. Guess what?"

They all leaned in closer as the reporter played along. "What?"

"David. Mr. Kelly, that is, told me the Secretary has a nickname for the President."

"Don't say? What might that be?"

The actress, enjoying the attention, continued to tease. "Guess what it is."

The reporter knew just what to say: "You can whisper it to me, so no one else hears. . ."

Monica whispered, 'The Southern Prince.' Isn't that the silliest?"

The reporter made a wrap motion to his cameraman as he answered. "Sure is, Annette . . . er, Monica . . . Walters, is it?"

"Waters. No 'L.' Of the 'The Gathering Storm.'"

David reached Monica as the reporters took their leave.

"Miss Waters. Thanks for the interview today."

"Interview?!" Monica had been enjoying the attention. Camera? Actress? Why on earth would she avoid a camera? Why, the whole world would soon know that she, Monica Waters, 'Annette' of 'The Gathering Storm,' had been in attendance at a Presidential news conference.

David realized too late what had happened. It wasn't Monica's fault. Hadn't he put her in the situation? What was she supposed to do? Reject publicity? Hide in her stunning white suit? Pretend that several cameras weren't trained directly on her? He may as well have asked her to perform electrical repair work. Shunning the spotlight simply wasn't part of Monica's DNA.

But it wasn't over yet. Suddenly the wall of reporters turned back to Monica following the tallest man in the room, who had decided to pay his respects. The President. His Secret Service officers even seemed to break concentration for a few moments.

David thought to himself, "There it is. If someone really wanted to take out the President, all that would be needed would be a Monica." She certainly had that effect on men. Shifted them right off their center of gravity.

Walker brushed by David, making a beeline for Monica. Soon, he found himself staring at an agent's back as he shielded the President. From him? He was the official here. Not Monica! Was Walker staring at her chest? David rejected the image and concentrated on their conversation instead.

"Why my goodness. If it isn't Annette."

"Oh, Mr. President. You know me?"

"The wife watches your show every day. You're here with . . .?"

At this question, David stepped forward. Finally, some attention. "David Kelly, sir. With Secretary Layton . . ."

Walker's eyes glanced over the agent's shoulder at David. He nodded briefly but turned back immediately. He had an important message to deliver. "Now then, my dear. I have a piece of advice for you . . ."

Monica looked like a deer caught in headlights. "Yes?"

"I want you to go on and have that little operation. You really must take better care of yourself. Also, dump Freddie. He's no good for you. . . ."

Monica was having trouble breathing. Walker noticed and placed a protective arm around her shoulder. "Now then, there, there. I tell you what? We will be needing for you to attend some events down in Washington."

At those words, he turned to one of the men, "Stan, get the lady's information, will you?"

David was stunned. Never had he seen a man, any man, much less the President, move so fast. In only a few minutes, he had made a pass at David's new girl-friend, revealing that he watched her show. And he had invited her to Washington. Later, when he could get Monica back down to earth over a cup of coffee, after her gushing about how tall Walker was, David got her to focus on her so-called 'interview.'

She was apologetic. She had not known they were taping it. Tears. Remorse. How could she possibly know what she had done? How could she know that her innocent remark would drive another nail in Layton's and David's coffins?

He put her in a cab with a kiss, and a promise to call. Then he made his way back to the hotel to inform Layton of the matter. Layton listened carefully, the line between his eyes deepening. Surprisingly, his reaction was resigned.

He sighed. "May as well go on and call Walker's press monkey. Fill them in. Better they should get it from us than to hear it later on cable news. Now see here, David. Do not give this a thought. We both know my banana peel's only good for about another six months. Maybe less. Either way, we'll be fine. We'll be fine."

As David left the room, he watched as Layton reached for a bottle of scotch from the mini-bar. Apparently, David wasn't the only one self-medicating lately.

He thought, "Just another day in New York City with Jeffrey Layton, the 'Southern Prince,' and 'Annette.'"

He wondered . . .

Did President Walker watch soap operas?

Was 'Annette' David's girlfriend?

Was Monica?

If fewer than fifteen days remained in 'month six,' could David now say, 'five months, and counting?'

Shouldn't he tell someone Japan had the bomb?

Would it be possible to locate 'Dream Girl' under the 'D's' in the phone book?

How exactly would United Airlines accommodate 35 live tropical fish – First Class, Business Class, or Aquarium Class?

Trouble was, he assigned the same importance to all of these questions. After he briefed a cranky presidential press aide, David wandered into a bar in Hell's Kitchen. There were still a couple of hours before train time. For now, 'The David Kelly School of Avoidance Therapy' would have to do.

CHAPTER TWENTY-EIGHT

Back home, although he had warned the White House of Monica's gaffe, David watched in amusement at their studied surprise as the story broke. There followed the inevitable 'highly placed source in the White House' leak about Secretary Layton's excessive travel. He was now being characterized as being 'off the reservation.'

Layton was now routinely described as the rogue cabinet member President Walker had molly-coddled too long. The White House branding and labeling work made David recall Layton's six-month deadline. Not only was it for real, it might come earlier. And if Layton was out, David was out.

Political animals that they were, they still hung poor Monica out to dry. She didn't mind taking the fall – they had a long talk about it, and she was eager to take the blame if it would make their lives easier. She really was a sweet woman.

There was also the 'law of unintended consequences to take into account.   Publicity surrounding the remark and Monica's televised 'interview' sent her show's ratings through the roof as viewers tuned in to check out the woman in the news. In no time, Monica's white suit was plastered across magazine covers and cable news shows.

How close was 'Annette' to the Commander in Chief?
Inquiring minds wanted to know. A cottage industry of tabloid stories
suddenly had Monica's agent working overtime, handling appearance
requests including an audition for a major Hollywood film.

Layton, to his credit, tried to get on the President's calendar to
smooth things over, but the winds blew cold from Pennsylvania
Avenue. Instead, he left for Japan again, assuring David that no one
needed to know of his personal trip.

When David wondered aloud if Nellie, his wife, would be going
along, he was sharply put in his place: "You are my legislative aide,
David. I do not believe that affords you the duties of confidential aide.
Now then, I'll be back in a few days. Keep an eye on the Hill. We need
that law now more than ever. Or six months will pass in so many days.
Got me?"

"Oh, yeah," David thought. "I've got you." David didn't need
Layton to draw him a picture. He already knew that when the Chief
Executive Officer of the damned country was angry with you, the door
could not be far away.

He fielded a sympathetic call from Julie, who had seen the news
reports. He spoke in vague generalities about his plans to move west.

But he didn't open up too much. She'd be tempted to say she told him so, and today he was in no mood. Even her silences, as in most long-term couples, spoke volumes. Volumes he could do without.

Part of her concern, he suspected was good old- fashioned green-eyed jealousy. She was wondering about Monica and himself. Well, let her wonder, he thought bitterly.

"Ernie Fields, his ass."

Two could play at this.

At the same time, part of him was pleased she still cared enough to care. "So, what?" was his next thought. So, what if she cares? What does that change? Then he answered his own question, "Absolutely nothing." All he needed to know was that he still liked redheads. Even if they were elusive. The right one would come along.

'Dream Girl.'

She would. Maybe he never did get that pony he wanted as a boy. But he was older now. More determined. More skilled. He would find her. Somewhere in Washington.

CHAPTER TWENTY-NINE

The next day, Saturday, dawned stormy and cold. To match his mood. Since it was still too early to have a drink, his "rule" being four o'clock, David decided to take a little trip downtown . . . to the Department of Resource Development . . . to Layton's office . . . to check things out a bit. He wore his trench coat for the weather and the mission.

The lobby guard recognized him and cleared him right through. Upstairs, another guard sat in the hallway near the Secretary's offices. He was watching a portable television. An old Warner Brothers film, "The Maltese Falcon," was playing. David could hear it as he entered the office.

Yes, sweetheart?

There's a girl to see you. Her name's Wandalay.

Customer?

I guess so. You'll want to see her anyway. She's a knock-out.

Show her in, Effie darling. Show her in.

As Bogart's voice rolled on, David sat at Marge's desk, and began going through her papers, opening drawers. He opened a ceramic rabbit that was on the shelf behind her desk. Keys! There was the sound of gunfire. For a moment, David stiffened until he realized it was just the TV.

Yeh. Speaking. Miles Archer, dead? Where? You're a detective, darling, but she didn't kill him.

Do the police really think you shot this what's his name? Do they? Look at me Sam. You worry me. You always think you know what you're doing. But you're too slick for your own good.

Hearing the words, David wondered, was that him? Nah. One thing he knew . . . he was not slick. He was nothing more than a scared government worker, trying to stay out of trouble long enough to clear town. He tried the keys. All he found were the usual files and letters. Local government officials asking for federal land use assistance. Normal stuff.

Then he recalled all the mysteries he had ever seen. Weren't the offending documents always behind a partition? He started to feel around Marge's desk. Did all the drawers go all the way back?

With a loud crack, the back part of one of the drawers came loose. David checked the guard. He was still engrossed in the movie.

May I offer my condolences for your partner's unfortunate death? . . . Is there, Mr. Spade, as the newspapers imply, a certain relationship between that, uh, unfortunate happening and, uh, the death a little later of the man Thursby?

David reached his hand behind the partition. He felt a canvas bag. As he pulled it out he could see the U.S. insignia. A diplomatic bag! He also saw the warning about tampering with U.S. property. "What the hell," thought David, as he broke through the seal. "In for a dime, in for a dollar."

Another lock. "Doesn't anyone trust anyone anymore?" David grinned at his own humor.

I am prepared to promise that, what is the phrase, no questions will be asked.

One of Marge's keys fit the lock. Eureka! He poured out the contents onto the desktop. U.S. dollars, about ten thousand, close as he could tell. A map of Japan, in Japanese. A U.S. Park Service pamphlet on fire prevention.

Unseen by David as he repacked the canvas bag was a button attached to the lining.

Unseen by him was the electronic signal that went out into the ether, beaming back to a distant office.

Unseen by David and Bogart both was a recorder that told someone somewhere of a break-in.

Of secrets spilled. And he was no closer to understanding anything. Just in a lot more trouble if he were found out.

Yes, Effie? No, that'll be all. Just be sure to lock the door behind you on your way out. Good night.

David replaced the bag and the desk partition. He tried to rearrange Marge's desk back to the way it was when he entered. Then he crept past the guard, by now taking himself a little Saturday nap. And out to the street below. He noticed how cold it was. How alone he felt. He scurried home to his fish and his fireplaces. He would call the boys. At least they were real.

CHAPTER THIRTY

It was mid-week, and David was left on his own. Layton, off on the mystery trip, called Marge, extending his time out of the office another four days. "God knows," thought David. "God knows."

Marge was in a more relaxed mood with the Secretary out of town, so the two went back to their old ways of kidding around. It was nice to lighten up for a change, David thought. She hadn't spoken of anything out of order on her desk. "How could she miss a broken lock on a diplomatic bag?" he wondered. Anyway, he wasn't about to ask.

"Leave well enough alone for a change," said the bird from his ledge.

He was to attend a key legislative meeting at the White House in Layton's place. Normally, such news would have been welcome. But David had already begun to emotionally distance himself from his job and the power perks that went along with it. That, and he had no idea what his reception over there might be, given the New York fiasco. Affiliation with Jeffrey Layton these days seemed to carry a certain onus where the executive branch was concerned.

As David entered the Executive Office Building –the "EOB," as
it was known locally -- he noticed Leon Barshevsky, President
Walker's Chief of Staff standing in a corner checking things out. From
time-to-time Barshevsky would nod at one of the guards or aides, and
they would race around complying with whatever – extra chairs, audio-
visual hook-ups, name tags.

David wondered at a person of such obvious power and position
using his time that way. Couldn't others concern themselves with such
minutiae? As David walked in, he had been on the receiving end of a
Barshevsky glare. "Fucking control freak," David thought. "Five
months and counting." He took his seat along with cabinet members
and other high-ranking officials for the briefing.

He took notes for the Secretary. The subjects ranged across the
Administration's policy objectives. The group was given the old "Rah!
Rah!" concerning the upcoming presidential election – it was not too
soon to preserve this president's legacy, not to mention his hold on the
power center of the free world. "Blah, blah, blah." David very nearly
nodded off. More than once, he felt his mind wandering to a list of
camping equipment he and the boys would need for their coming trip to
St. John's.

Finally, it was over, and he walked outside into a beautiful
sunny winter's day. As he was putting on his sunglasses, his cell phone

rang. It was Marge and she sounded frantic to reach him. He was to return home immediately. There was some sort of flood involving his apartment. David's Foggy Bottom place was only six blocks from the White House-EOB complex.

As he raced home, he was thankful the emergency was simply having to do with a building, and not one of his sons. As the father of two active boys, David already had had his share of hospital emergency rooms, and doctors stitching active bodies back together.

When he arrived, his doorman was in a state. His French accent had grown thicker as he attempted to describe the problem to David. All he could make out was the word 'flood.' When he got to his floor, he was greeted by pandemonium. The hall carpet was soaked. His front door stood wide open, and various building engineers were already inside with towels and cleaning implements.

The situation grew worse as he entered his apartment. His prize fish were strewn over the living room carpet amidst shards of broken glass from the aquarium, What the hell? Aquariums didn't explode for no reason. The entire scene was hard to grasp.

As he stepped over his yellow Long-Nosed Butterfly Fish, his Lipstick Tang, and a black-finned Triggerfish, he felt his stomach turn over. He didn't even wish to pick them up. They were lifeless anyway, their saltwater colors as stunning as ever. What the hell had happened here?

The police showed up soon afterwards. Then, a detective. Later, an insurance man from the building. Finally, his downstairs neighbor, whose apartment also was soaked. No one was happy. David was numb. He just stood in the middle of the room, staring at the scene.

Finally, the detective asked him to join him in the hallway. Quietly, he asked if he had any enemies. Shocked, David answered none. "Well," the detective whispered, "someone did this to you. We found bullet holes in the side of the tank and through the wall behind. Someone entered with a key and shot out your tank. This was no accident."

He took the man's card and promised to call if he could remember anyone who might have it in for him. The man warned him, "You can have the locks changed. But I have to tell you, whoever did this to you entered with a key."

At some level, David heard him. He signed some building forms, and the insurance report. He listened as the building manager assured him in no uncertain terms that none of the staff had been in his unit that day. He apologized to his downstairs neighbor. It seemed the right thing to do, even though it wasn't his fault. He gave the crew permission to gather up the dead fish and glass and air out the area. As the men went about their work, he mixed himself a drink.

Hours seemed to pass. Finally, he was left alone. His doors and windows stood open, the heat was turned up, and fans were positioned to speed along the drying process. He made himself another drink. Stared at his kitchen wall for a while.

And then he remembered something. The blinking light on the bag. What if someone had tracked his movements? Knew about his search. And had just delivered him a warning. Today, his fish. Tomorrow, what?

He put his head in his hands. He cried for his handsome fish. They were such beauties. And he kept crying. For his boys. His marriage. For a widow left alone due to a senseless tragedy. For a country led by a man who threw furniture. For his life in a shambles.

His tears, of course, changed nothing. But they set him on a new course. He no longer needed a reason to alter his life. He knew nothing would be the same. He was heading into uncharted waters. And that was not necessarily a bad thing.

In the meantime, he called a locksmith.

CHAPTER THIRTY-ONE

Dulles International Airport

Warnings. David had received more than his share lately. Of course, each bore the characteristic of deniability. Each occurrence, if considered alone, would be a sign only of his own paranoia. Taken together? They began to add up to one clear response: a one-way ticket back to Seattle. Away from it all. To a liveaboard lifestyle with 'Dream Girl.' And his boys.

David was not the only one reading tea leaves. The assassin, Frank, to his friends, also was being warned.

Dulles International Airport is always a busy place. Many international entries and exits. Tight customs control. Carefully monitored passages. One international flight by a small South American carrier was dead-heading, returning a non-revenue jet that had been repaired down south. Part of the plane's tail section had flown off in a hurricane some months earlier.

The plane's crew passed through their own customs gate upon arrival in Virginia. One member of the crew fell ill just before takeoff. His place onboard was taken by a new crew member no one knew.

They were told he had been hired out of the New York office. The new man was in company uniform, and his passport and entry papers were in order.

Seated out of earshot from the others, the assassin, Frank, to his friends, placed a cell phone call to his wife, who was on her way to the airport to meet him. She was bursting with good news. Their son had been responding well to the new experimental cancer treatment during the time he'd been away. The boy's hair was growing back; his appetite was returning. Together, the parents rejoiced, planning a family celebration dinner.

Later, on the ground, as they walked to the family station wagon, his wife delivered another piece of news. His partner on former missions, including the Lechman affair, had been killed in Europe. He had been the victim of a single-car crash on the German Autobahn. Reports were that he had not been wearing a seatbelt.

Immediately, Frank, to his friends knew the story was just that, a story. He had carried out over thirty missions with this man. His partner was one of the most methodical, cautious men he knew. No way would he have gone out that way. Someone had given him a bit of a shove.

And he knew full well what that meant: Frank had moved up in an exclusive queue known only to a few. The queue consisted of men who knew too much. Men who had been there, seen the action. Because there was a shelf life to this line of work. Handlers would want to be sure. Once enough services were rendered, at some point a man would need to be 'retired.'

Trouble was that their idea of 'retirement' was not other people's. Their version had widows receiving lifetime pensions. Children being covered by medical insurance. Houses being saved, mortgages being paid up. And the fathers? Gone, in tragic accidents. Buried with military honors. Don't ask, don't tell.

Frank knew it was time to activate his plan. This was one assassin who intended to live to a ripe old age in a far-off land. With his family by his side. First, however, he had a final lesson for his handlers. "Fool me once, shame on you. Fool me twice, I'll be dead," he thought grimly.

As the ordinary looking family station wagon made its way to the Dulles Access Road, Frank, to his friends was heavy in thought. He had ample evidence of other colleagues who had met untimely ends. What did he need, a picture painted?

He planned to break the pattern. He would leave all right.

But when he did, it would be on his terms, not some shit handler's.

CHAPTER THIRTY-TWO

. . . Elsewhere at Dulles International Airport . . .

"Oh, it's a snug little island! A right little, tight little island."
The Snug Little Island, by Thomas Dibdin

It was an odd little crew that assembled prior to takeoff in the
V.I.P. lounge at Virginia's Dulles Airport. Sybil, the group's hostess,
bustled about making sure her guests had drinks and snacks. Already
ensconced were her and Horace's close friends from Middleburg, Leila
and Steven Harumi. The Secretary had just arrived, on time for a
change.

They were awaiting the party's last two guests. Because they
were flying on the Lechman plane, departure time could pretty much be
whenever they damned well pleased, with deference paid only to the
many international jumbo jets flying in and out. Still, there was a large
degree of control and luxury to the Lechman form of travel.

Sybil was called to the telephone as her fourth guest, 'Dear
Boy,' arrived, still slightly taken aback at his inclusion in such a party.
David was gratified by Sybil's unexpected invitation to spend a long
week-end at her sumptuous home in Montego Bay.

She had couched the invitation in her usual 'Lavender Lady' candor.

"Now see here. I, for one, recognize unhappiness when I see it. You qualify. Therefore, you will join us for a relaxing week-end, no agendas. No work. No cares. It is the very least I can offer you for your many kindnesses."

What could he say? And so, bag in hand, a chino-clad David joined the estimable jet-set in the lounge. As he entered the lounge, a steward pressed a mimosa cocktail into his hand and took his luggage to the cart. Layton, deep in conversation with Steven Harumi, nodded in his direction.

David recognized the Harumi's from their frequent appearances in the Post's Style Section. Close friends of the President, they were front and center at the town's key social events. Leila Harumi, a shining past-middle aged blonde loaded with heirloom diamonds, warmly welcomed him as Sybil took her call.

Soon, their disappointed hostess returned to the group, announcing that her fifth guest was unable to make the trip due to a flare-up in her recently broken leg. A steward quietly removed a wheelchair positioned in the corner.

"Fiddle-dee-dee. That makes us uneven at dinner. Can't be helped. Broken legs can be quite incapacitating, I know. We shall simply have to overcome our disappointment with one more drink, kind steward, before we board."

With that, the group bravely suffered the prospect of an uneven dinner number with more libations, served in crystal glasses wrapped in linen napkins, as they boarded the Lechman jet.

The hostess had somehow failed to mention to David that 'Guest Number Five' had been a 'fix up' intended for him . . . that the guest in question was an attractive red-head with a braid reaching to a trim waist, and a sprinkle of girlish freckles across an upturned nose.

Sybil knew men. Especially depressed ones. They were flighty and unpredictable, ready to bolt at the slightest noise. David, as she knew, already was operating from a precarious ledge. So, her fix-up had been foxily planned.

The young woman, who was managing the store opening Sybil was chairing, also was a nervous creature. Upon meeting her, Sybil instantly thought of 'Dear Boy.' The two, in her estimation, would make a fine pair – two skittish middle-aged adults, scared out of their wits of commitment. Each had their reasons. But to Sybil those reasons added up to only one thing: They would make the perfect match.

She had performed this service for others in the past. Her superior powers of observation rarely failed her. The woman had lived a full life, filled with lovers, husbands, poverty, and great wealth -- circumstances so varied, she had developed the uncanny ability to read people for who they really were.

She could peer beneath people's masks. This ability had been tremendously helpful to her Horace. She watched out for him -- her big man. When he was preoccupied with facts and figures, Sybil went to town. It was her business to know and know she did.

As she took her seat at the front of the luxurious plane, she made a mental note to find another way. 'Dear Boy' and 'Skittery' were on a collision course of love so far as she was concerned. And Sybil rarely took no for an answer.

Clueless as to his close call with an attractive redhead, David boarded the private plane carrying his refilled cocktail glass. What a strange new world this was. A table was set for dinner towards the rear of the plane, he noticed.

"What the hell. May as well live a little," David thought.

He had packed a new snorkel mask to try out for his trip later with the boys. "Beats dunking it in the tub at home," he thought, as he settled into a reclining padded seat. The seat came equipped with his own reading lamp, snacks, and television monitor. Fresh flowers hung in a vase on the wall overhead. What was that scent? Lavender. The plane's ventilation system overrode the smell of jet fuel. The sound of the engines revving for take-off was about the only familiar thing about the trip so far.

David observed the others as they settled in. Soon, the plane lifted effortlessly into the Virginia sunset and headed south to the ocean. He could see the lights twinkle along the coastline below as night took over. Soon they were served a superb French meal, rivaling any David had had on the ground. Even the rolls were fresh and still warm from the oven. A delicate parsley and wine sauce touched perfectly done salmon steaks. The salad with chunks of bleu cheese and sweet cherry tomatoes was served later.

Back in his seat, David's workaday world fell away. Soon enough he was enjoying an after-dinner drink and reading his book. He was no match, however, for the fine meal and wine. Soon, his head fell against the designer cushion. A steward quietly removed his tray and placed a robe monogrammed with a Lechman Industries logo around him.

The sudden turbulence of an island landing awakened him. He was the only one awake. The Secretary was sound asleep, a black nightshade over his eyes. The cabin lights were dimmed. The plane stumbled and lurched through the night. David had never been particularly fearful of flying, however tonight he felt very alone with these strangers onboard a strange plane, bound for some island.

"What was he doing here?" he thought, as his book tumbled to the floor of the aircraft. A steward, noticing he was awake, brought him a glass of sparkling water and a steamy hot face cloth.

"Normal bumps, sir. We always get this on this side of the island. Soon as the plane turns back, it'll smooth back out again."

No sooner had he said the words than the plane turned, levelled off and made a quick, smooth descent and landing. Within ten minutes the executive jet was on the ground, and David's fellow passengers were rousing themselves. The crew already had boarded and removed luggage to the waiting van. Once again, David could not remember de-planing without carrying a single item. He was in capable hands. Never had surrender been this easy.

With a soft island breeze blowing through the van's open windows, the guests were driven to the highest point overlooking the

Bay. The Lechman estate was located at the end of a long drive that had lush jungle foliage and tiki lights along the way.

When they arrived, David watched with amusement the by-play between Sybil and the Secretary.

"Jeffrey, I am taking this damned phone away, and you may have it back later. This is supposed to be a vacation. The nation will survive."

With those words, Sybil grabbed Layton's phone and dropped it in the koi pond next to the van. To David's surprise, Layton seemed to enjoy the rough treatment, leaning over to give his demanding hostess a kiss on the cheek. Sybil responded by rubbing up against him. The widow seemed to be recovering, David noted.

Soon, David was escorted to a perfect little beach cabana overlooking the Bay. He had his own lanai, was shown the drink cart, guest robe and slippers, and a call list of services available to him 24-7. He noted he could have any type of food or drink, a whirlpool spa, a massage, a yoga class, or a sailing lesson. He opened the lanai doors wide before settling between the ironed, silky white sheets for the best sleep he could remember having in months.

When he awoke, David had no idea what time it was, but the sun seemed to be well up in the sky. Embarrassed, he quickly showered and put on a pair of island shorts and shirt and hurried over to the main house. A staff member ushered him to the back-porch dining area. There, Sybil, still in her robe, was reading the island newspaper. A full buffet was laid out, and the smell of fresh-roasted coffee and baked bread gave him an appetite.

"David, my dear. Come right in and have something to eat. The men have been exiled. I sent them to play golf. They were getting on my nerves. ."

David could tell his hostess was in her element, commandeering her adoring guests. So that was how it was going to be? Like Layton the night before, David quickly surrendered to her mothering. In an odd sort of way, it was nice, being ordered around, not having to make his own decisions.

'Dear Boy,' in from the ledge.

Temporarily.

The Widow continued on as he gobbled sweet fresh mango.

"I hope you don't mind. Oh, and Leila has gone off shopping. Her favorite thing, I can attest. So, do make yourself at home. I can tell you I am simply exhausted. The funeral and all. So, I plan on not dressing the entire day. So there. My, how handsome you are in the light. Oh, please don't be embarrassed. I am, I am afraid, overly frank with people. Horace always told me I ought to dial it down a bit. You, for instance. I have felt a certain simpatico from the beginning. Have you felt it?"

She didn't give him even a moment to respond.

"Do not ask me why. Just a feeling. Now then. This is your day, my dear. No structure. Dinner's at 8. We dress for dinner here. Gowns. Jewels. The whole nine yards. But until then? Go native! The less clothing, the better!"

With that, the Widow refilled her own coffee cup and headed off to another part of the house, their conversation apparently ended. David continued his island breakfast with eggs and bacon. Then more fresh fruit. And several more cups of coffee. He glanced at 'The Islander,' the local paper Sybil had been reading. There had been a murder onboard a charter yacht moored in the harbor. The article hinted at drugs, and by the size of the headline, it was clear news rarely penetrated this island's serenity.

When he was finished, he was whisked to the beach by a staff member along with instructions on where to be for his massage later in the day. What a curious experience it all was. And David was enjoying every moment.

His afternoon consisted of dips in the ocean, flight-testing the snorkel, sunbathing, and the massage. Someone even came into his cabana to give him a pedicure, his first. What luxury! He took a long cool bath, tried to read a mystery novel, took a nap and then woke to a musical tune playing on his phone.

"It's seven o'clock, Mr. Kelly. Dinner's at eight," a disembodied voice instructed.

Rolling over, David came eyeball to eyeball with a creature sitting on his bed. A toucan had hopped into the cabana and was busily staring at the sleeping human.

"Welcome to the islands," he seemed to be saying.

Heeding Sybil's directive to dress for dinner, David took care with his preparations. He was glad he had thought to pack a pair of summer weight linen slacks, brightly colored Hawaiian shirt, and blazer jacket. "Dear Boy" looked at his reflection in the mirror. A rested version of himself stared back. Washington, D.C. seemed very far away tonight.

As he walked up the path to the main house, tiki lights lit his way. Inside, the house was glowing, and he heard soft jazz music playing as he was shown into the library. He was the last to arrive and took a moment to appreciate the scene. A fire crackled in the large stone fireplace, soft candlelight reflected off of the mirrors and fine paintings.

The women were beautiful, their substantial jewels catching the firelight. Bouquets of island flowers were banked everywhere, the stewards served from silver trays. All in all, it was an exquisite scene.

Everyone appeared rested and happy. Crystal glasses held wonderful island rum drinks, and waiters in white jackets passed trays of marinated shrimp. The conversation warmed as second and third rounds of drinks moved the group towards the elegant dinner table. 'Social Layton' treated David as a peer. He in no way acted as his boss, giving David a break from their normal routine.

At dinner, David was seated next to Leila Harumi, and discovered her to be a delightful dinner companion. The woman was extremely well-read and held her own as they engaged in a lengthy discussion of the world's environment. He enjoyed her bubbly sense of humor and could feel the effects of the wine making the evening spin into a dream of gaiety and high spirits. He knew his dinner partner played a large role in his sense of ease. No wonder the Harumi's were such sought after social denizens. They both had a studied grace and charm that made them the perfect dinner companions.

The dinner meandered slowly through the island evening. Waiters brought new wines for each course. By the time the bananas flambé arrived with coffee, Sybil suggested they take their desserts and coffee on the large lanai, open to the ocean waves crashing below. She received no arguments.

Once they were comfortable, she and Layton took their leave back to the den. David noticed her shoo a waiter out as she firmly closed the heavy wooden doors behind them. He would have given a half year's salary to hear what the two were discussing. Instead, he settled for more time spent with the Harumi's. Eventually, Steven Harumi nodded off in his chair. Leila roused him and they made their goodnights.

David was left alone on the veranda. A man came to bring him more coffee and also shut the windows, making the porch strangely silent. Except for . . . the sound of Sybil's voice. Suddenly, David could overhear the two, unnoticed. The evening for him had ended, and he should have returned to his cabana. Instead, he motioned for another coffee and strained to hear their conversation. He only got snatches – Sybil's voice carried better than Layton's. What little he got was disturbing.

". . . murdered. . . no accident. . . Matthew was. . needed . . . reelection campaign. . . withdraw his support . . ."

Layton's voice rose briefly, "What on earth do you expect me to do about it, dear lady?! You are accusing . . ." Then the voices grew quiet.

David had heard enough. He quickly scurried out of the big house into the tropical night, his island calm now gone. The bird was back on his ledge, more worried than ever. Thoughts crowded his mind. The man-in Japan .. Horace . . . his murdered fish . . . the diplomatic bag . . .a President's temper . . . Who'd believe any of it?

As David undressed and slipped between the bed covers, back at the house, the conversation took many twists and turns.

Sybil presented Layton with her proof. Layton read Horace's long letter as carefully as Sybil herself had. She tried to speak, but Layton's raised hand stopped her. He re-read parts of the letter. Then he took a moment to collect his thoughts before leveling a dispassionate lawyerly gaze upon The Widow.

"What did you have in mind?"

Sybil had not experienced the all-business Layton before. She found this side of him at once comforting and disturbing.

"I have gone over it and over it in my mind. I have called my attorneys. At a minimum, I want Horace's money back. Oh, not for myself, you understand. I have what I need. But for his children, his grandchildren, his causes. Not for Matthew Walker and his kind. Not for them. Never again for them."

Layton's response was harsh, even challenging.

"On what grounds would you go after the money? This letter? The confused ramblings of an elderly man at the end of his career who put his faith in the wrong man?!"

Sybil began to cry softly. "Oh, Jeffrey. Help me. Please, for the love of God, help me."

"Attention must be paid. You would need far more proof. My God, woman, are you actually considering taking on the President of the United States on the basis of some supposition you have no way of proving?"

He continued. "Horace's boat exploded. There was virtually nothing left. Who was at the sight? His people. Do you think anything was preserved? Any evidence? No, now, now . . . don't get me wrong. I believe Horace. Even from the grave, he is a powerful presence. But Matthew Walker .. I could tell you things . . . President? Dictator's more like it. A tin-pot one at that. Ever since he brought in that schnauzer Barshevsky, things have been going down hill. Horace had it right. Money has superseded any pretense of morality in this administration."

Now the flood gates were open. "I am ashamed of my part in all of it. Hell, woman! What do you think I have been doing, gallivanting around the globe? Carrying bags of cash for the Southern Prince. And what is offered in return? I used to think, world peace, in its fashion. I could tell you what they told me, honorable payments for honorable needs. Now . . . now, I'm not so sure."

Sybil watched Layton as he broke cabinet silence and confirmed Horace's worst suspicions. Until now, she had held out some hope that her man was wrong. Not now. Not now. She refocused on her friend as he finished: " . . . not covered by our Constitution, I can tell you. No, dear lady, what we are facing is pure evil. No less than pure evil. Let's give it its proper name!"

"Oh, Jeffrey!"

Layton crossed the room and took Sybil in his arms. He brought her gently back to the couch in front of the fire. They sat close. He took her hand in his own and continued, quieter now.

"Until I read Horace's letter, I imagined myself a paranoid old fool. I knew Walker had a lousy environmental record. I had no illusions about that. He needed my reputation to add to his team. I always thought it was a fair trade – my good name for the chance to do things at a higher level . . ."

Sybil could tell that what Layton was about to share would be important. She listened carefully to this man whose counsel and friendship she so desperately needed.

"You know how we all felt about Matthew back a few years. Horace, his strongest supporter. And for good reason. The promise of greatness. The idealism. The stamina. You both saw it – a charming renaissance man capable of protecting the interests of business and the environment at the same time. But a man with global vision, who could relate Detroit car sales to weather patterns in the Saharan Desert. As the saying goes, "A man for all seasons." So, what the hell happened? Where in the Sam Hill did our Matt Walker go to?"

Sybil knew the answer, but she could not share it with Jeffrey. She understood Matthew Walker because she understood herself.

Unlike Layton, she, Horace and Matthew each came from the underside of America's middle class. All had parlayed physical and mental advantages to break the glass ceiling of class. All had clawed their way into it. But it wasn't enough. Because there were always questions. Always slights.

Discrimination of any kind is best understood by experience. Sybil knew Jeffrey's life had always been charmed. Hers, Horace's, and Matthew's had not been. Their lives had been composed of grit, determination, a bit of acting, and knowing when to turn the other cheek. These things she knew. These things she would not share with her friend tonight.

But as he continued, Sybil realized she had sold him short.

"It has to do with upbringing. Take a look at his early years. He came from nothing. Raised around an alcoholic father, a mother of questionable morals. Then this estimable kid finds himself in the world of wealth. He develops a taste for it. The fine art. The custom-tailored shirts. The private jets. The trust fund crowd. People who have never known a day of want in their lives. . . ."

Layton continued.

"And as he rose and grew closer to that set, two things became apparent. No matter how high up he got, he'd never be one of them. You know the rules. You can have money. That part's allowed. But they will never let you in. Not really."

Sybil thought, "And you, dear Jeffrey?" But as soon as she had the thought she realized how very unique was her Jeffrey. The young man who had gone to the mountain top to meditate. The young man who somehow had managed to keep his wits and his soul together in a brutal world.

Then she reminded him, "And the second thing?"

"An overwhelming desire never to be poor again."

As she spoke, Sybil knew Jeffrey was right. "But he won't be."

"Ah, dear lady. It's no longer just about the money. By now it's an addiction. The power. The whole scene. There is no perspective now. Things have gone out of control. Problem is, not so's the general public can notice. To them, he's still the fair-haired boy with an answer for every question. Still one of the most popular presidents this country has ever known. And if you and your lawyers set out after him . . .?" At this Layton shook his head.

"I don't care. I want that money returned. Whatever it takes. And I want the man driven from office. If Horace really did die by his hand, I want that man out!"

One of the reasons Sybil loved Jeffrey Layton so much was because of his realism and his desire always to do the right thing. Few men of his station could claim such strong characters. Her Horace, of course. No other men she knew. Now a steady hand took the tiller. She could not ignore his seriousness. Could not question his motivation.

"Dear lady. What we want and what we get will be two different things, I am afraid. And we do not really know, can never really know, whether or not Matthew had a hand in this. Now then. Hear me carefully. Because what I am about to say is extremely important."

Sybil was tiring of this. Her shoulders ached from the tenseness of it all. A man came to adjust the fire, but she waved him away.

"Safety. That is my concern now. Silence and safety. The two go hand in hand, you know. You, dear lady, will call those damned lawyers of yours back when we return to town. D'they see the letter yet?"

Sybil nodded no.

"That's good. That's good. Now here's what I want you to do. Tell the men that you were distraught when you called before. Not yourself. You were beside yourself with grief, you were lashing out at anyone you could. In short, you will lie. You will retreat. You will never see this money. You should not pursue it."

He continued: "The best I can offer you is never to vote for Matthew Walker again. That, so far as we know, is a privilege you may still enjoy. Vote for his opponent, no matter how bad. Turn him out of office. That is your only course of action. Now, then, have I made myself clear?"

Sybil nodded her head as she buried her face against her friend's shoulder. She was tired now. She had her answer. She had sought information from one of the best. He had only her interests at heart, no question. The counsel was given, and it was valued.

But doubts lingered. Feelings not so easily dispensed with. Not so soon. Not yet. But she nodded all the same. Out of respect for her friend. For his sincerity. His gravitas. Layton was a loyal friend.

But she knew friendship was not the only matter on the table tonight. She also needed to think of her Horace. He was her primary concern. Not even her own safety preceded his memory. Horace had spoken. Sybil would not soon forget.

"... *murdered*... *no accident*. ... *Matthew was* ... *needed*... *reelection campaign*. .. *withdraw his support* ... "

Back at the cabana, the island winds picked up and "Dear Boy" slept on through the night.

CHAPTER THIRTY-THREE

Kuma Station, Hokkaido Japan, 1967

In the spring of 1967, there was a 7-point 8 earthquake centered at Aomori on Honshu's northern coast. The quake was so powerful that it rocked the entire island of Hokkaido to the north. The ground moved laterally three feet in a slow, see-sawing motion. After that, the ground took on a rolling motion like a ship at sea.

A psychic had predicted that an island in the Pacific would sink that very year, making Americans on the island more than a little nervous. Some thought the active volcano, Mt. Taramai, would somehow be triggered and bring them all down to an ocean abyss. GI's stationed at Kuma Station ran from their barracks naked, then requested a change of station to Vietnam. "At least there, you know who's shooting at you," went the logic.

This U.S. military base was an Army Security Agency outpost, predating satellite eavesdropping technology. At Kuma Station, Chinese and Russian linguists translated all air traffic picked up from that part of the world. Hokkaido's strategic location was just south of Russia's test base, the Sakhalin Islands, and within range of China and Korea.

Pilots' conversations were transcribed, and essential military information was transmitted through a series of siftings back to Washington, D.C. Russian moon launches were monitored. The men's motto, 'Forewarned is Cheating,' appeared on jacket patches and tee shirts with a picture of an American Eagle with tennis shoes and a head-set listening at a keyhole. The slogan summed up the mission at this remote outpost: No matter where on earth you are, the United States is listening.

On occasion, deep-sea nuclear testing was conducted in the vicinity of Hokkaido. Only the men, sworn to secrecy, knew who was doing the testing. The official story was Russia. Partly true. The other part was Japan. Japan, the non-nuclear country, under the cover of "Mother Russia," was conducting their own underground nuclear tests.

Shh. Don't ask, don't tell.

For many years, the mutual silence club had dictated that America would quietly watch all testing. She also watched the disposal of nuclear waste product. In Japan's case, a small land mass meant they needed to find another country for their dumping. China was ruled out – they hated and feared them. Korea, same story.

The only other country in the area was Russia, and they were in an ongoing territorial dispute over the Sakhalin Islands. However, necessity being the mother of invention, Japan made their deal. Barged their waste north. To Russia. For years, this seemed to work. Russia was not exactly known as the center of all environmental regard.

After the many leadership changes in Russia, however, some Russian generals threatened to go public with Japan's dirty little secret. 'International diplomacy,' solved the problem. The arrangement was renegotiated to another country.

Under Matthew Walker's guidance, 'The Eagle' agreed to accept Japan's waste on the 'down low.' In exchange for certain remunerations to his personal account. 'The Wilderness President' had some wilderness for sale. The deal was made. And guaranteed.

Leon Barshevsky counted the money.

CHAPTER THIRTY-FOUR

"If all be true that I do think, There are five reasons we should drink:
Good wine – a friend – or being dry – Or lest we should be by and by – Or any other
reason why."
Five Reasons for Drinking, by Henry Aldrich

". . . murdered. . . no accident. . . Matthew was . . . needed . . .
reelection campaign. . . withdraw his support . . ."

Back home, Sybil's words re-ran in David's mind. One minute,
he was James Bond, solving a mystery. The next, his common sense
kicked in.

"Calm the hell down," he told himself. "Sybil is a flighty
woman of a certain age who misses her husband and wants someone to
pay for his death. It's not your problem."

But the mere accumulation of detritus facts had David reaching
for the bottle more and enjoying it less. Emotionally speaking, he
already was a wreck long before the break-in at his home. Unknown
intruders entering his personal environment with their own key . . .
what was that about?

As he arrived home, the memory of his colorful tropical fish lying dead all over the living room carpet wouldn't go away. The mess had been cleaned up, the glass shards carted off, the rug dried out. He had restocked the aquarium shelf with books. Still, the wall where his beautiful fish once lived was the first place he looked to on arriving home, and the last place he checked when he left.

Alcohol was an interim solution to his deteriorating state of mind. Not the solution, he was aware. There was an Irish pub near Union Station. He found himself spending more time there, avoiding that bookshelf at home. He stopped off after work. What harm could there be in that?

Many people lived their lives like that. Desperation kept at bay on a daily maintenance regimen. If one were disinclined to introspection, there was a variety of addictions available. David chose one of the more popular choices – a good, stout pint.

". . . murdered. . . no accident. . . ."

It was a Thursday evening. In the shadow of Capital Hill, David was walking to the pub on his way home. A drunken woman sidled up to him, nodding her head in the direction of the Capital Dome.

"Used to work up there."

" . . . no accident. . . . Matthew was . ."

"You did?"

"Yep. For a big man. The biggest. All he took from the people was cash. Cold cash."

"Who'd you work for?"

" . . reelection campaign. . . withdraw his support . . ."

"Ah, young man like yourself. You wouldn't know him. Anyway, he's long dead now. Long dead."

"What'd you do for him?"

"Letters mostly. Some shopping. Bought his wife's Christmas presents several years in a row."

David began walking faster as the light changed. He looked over his shoulder at the woman.

"That so . . ."

"Someone entered with a key and shot out your tank. This was no accident."

He approached the front door of the pub, with the woman close behind. As he entered, the woman trailed him. A waiter began to shoo her out the door, but David interrupted him.

"She's with me. We'll have a couple of drafts."

Seated, the woman self-consciously wiped her dirty hands on a napkin. She continued her story, as though there had been no interruption.

"That year it snowed. Real deep, it was. You're a good man. A real friend."

" Friendship's important." The drinks arrived, and each took satisfying sips. The woman's sip lasted half the mug, he noted.

"So, you make a habit of buying people off the streets, drinks, mister? Something's off with you."

David thought, "Something's off with you!"

Instead, he said, "And you are . . . the CIA?"

"Far from it. Hey, but I think they might'a followed me around once upon a time. To get some stuff on the congressman . . ."

"The CIA? Sure, it wasn't the KGB?"

The two kept talking through two more mugs of beer.

"Ah, go ahead and laugh. Looks of you, you could use a laugh. What's wrong, buddy? It's big ain't it?"

" . .entered with a key . . ."

"Someone has been doing some traveling for the President, let us say . . ."

"Not the first time. That's how it's done."

"What's done?"

"Go on."

"Been a lot in the newspapers about these trade deals lately. Basically good. Shepherding scarce resources, creating jobs for people, that sort of stuff . . ."

"Yeh, yeh. I read the P.R. too."

"It seems that, along the way, well, of course, anyone knows, campaigns cost. TV ads run in the millions these days . . ."

"Uh-huh."

"Seems some Japanese sources have taken quite an interest in the election. To the tune of a lot of money. 'Course there's a quid pro quo. Can't say. Can't say. Sh-hh! It's a secret."

"Oh sure. A secret. You ain't with the Pentagon. This we know."

David had had enough. He bought her some drinks. Fun's over. He rose to leave.

"Well, look, ma'am. I'd better be going now. Still have lots to do tonight."

The woman blocked David's path. Suddenly, she sounded sober.

"Now then, you listen to me, mister. This time you got lucky. You had a few drinks with a woman who can't hurt you. Luck doesn't hit twice, especially in this town. Got me?"

David laughed and attempted to place his hand on her shoulder. "You're my friend."

"No such thing in Washington. Get yourself a dog."

"I had a buncha fish . . ."

"Can't talk to fish. A dog. That's the ticket."

The two walked outside, and the woman disappeared around a corner. As David turned towards Union Station, a Town Car pulled up. It was "CJ," Layton's driver.

"Hey, Kelly! Need a ride?"

"Thanks, CJ. I could use one. It's been a long week."

"Well, you did start it on some Caribbean island . . . oh, yes. That's right. We know all about your little trip. You'd be surprised what goes around the Department . . . but hey, I know what you mean, about being tired, I mean. My daughter was in her first, and I hope, her last, car accident this week. She's drivin' with her little friends. She's talkin' on her cell. She's not watchin', needless to say. And 'Boom!.' Some guy hits her. Lucky it was the SUV, or she'd be hurt. Never, I tell you never, give a teenager the car keys!"

"I hear you. Glad she's okay though."

David's thoughts turned to Josh and Kenny. Three more years and they would be bugging him for their learners' permits. Then college. Marriage. . . . The big car pulled up to the Hart Senate Office Building. Layton stepped in, surprised to see David.

"Well, well. Looks like I'm taking the local tonight. Good to see you, David."

CJ asked, "Any stops tonight sir?"

David said, "Uh, CJ offered me a ride home. Hope you don't mind."

There was a nervous silence as the two men sized each other up. Layton wanted to talk with David; David wanted to talk with Layton. Neither man wanted to begin. Each knew that to begin, they would also need to finish. And they didn't much care for where such a conversation might lead.

David, with four beers under his belt, began.

"Mr. Secretary . . ."

"CJ, Kelly's coming with me to the house first, then you can drop him back to town. David, you can call me Jeffrey. It's after hours now."

"Jeffrey. I have wanted to have a personal conversation with you . . . ever since the last one we had . . . then on the island, there never seemed the right time . . ."

"I know, I know. Quite the woman, our Sybil. Taken quite a shine to you, I can say. Watch out now. She is a very demanding presence. Once Sybil is in your life, she's in your life, if you catch my meaning."

David did.

Layton lowered his voice. "We'll talk back at the house."

With that, he turned on his reading light, a signal there would be no more conversation in the car. The men rode in silence down a busy M Street in Georgetown and then out along the river to one of

Washington's prestige addresses, Potomac, Maryland, home to cabinet members, diplomats, and other arrivistes.

Once inside the large colonial style home, Layton waved off his wife and escorted David into the study. He fixed himself a drink and offered one to David.

"Geez, my life's become an alcoholic nightmare!" he thought, as he accepted the gin and tonic. Suddenly wanting to feel and remain sober, the bird on the ledge only pretended to sip the drink. Layton wasn't noticing anyway.

Layton began.

"Good time in Montego?"

"Sure. It was great. Interesting woman, Sybil."

He had hit on one of Layton's favorite subjects, The Widow. Here was a woman, it was clear, who wouldn't remain a widow for long, if Layton had anything to say about it.

"Guess you're wondering . . . about Nellie, I mean . . ."

"Frankly sir, I have always imagined that to be none of my affair."

"Rightly so. Rightly so. Still and all, I have dragged you a-ways further into this than I might have intended. Sybil enjoys your company. She tells me she 'gets you,' whatever the Sam Hill that means."

"She imagines us kindred spirits, two unhappy people, is all."

Layton refreshed his drink. "Guess you know you came that close to a fix up this past week-end. I've actually met the woman. Red hair, beautiful. Wears it in one of those long braids down her back . . ."

At this, he had David's full and undivided attention. He tried to appear nonchalant. "She's, uh, working with Sybil on this store opening?"

"Yes. Yes. Hails from Portland, of all places. Thirty-something. Excellent marketer, according to Sybil. Piss poor on politics however. Which is where our lady comes in. From all those years with Horace, she knows everyone in this town and can put together a guest list like nobody's business. Uh, about Nellie . . ."

"Listen, sir, I really don't have to . . ."

Layton ran right over David's words. "There is no spark. With Sybil, well, with Sybil, it's the goddamned Fourth of July. Listen, Nellie and me've had ourselves a pretty good run. She will make out very well on what I am prepared to settle. But see here, I simply wanted to thank you for your, er, for your, well . . . your discretion."

"Sure, no problem."

The two sat in silence. Layton clearly had had his say. If David wanted any more information, he sensed it would be a long wait. Still, he needed to take his shot. He began carefully.

"I have a confession to make."

Layton now eyed him carefully.

"We have had quite a list of strange things happen lately. Do you agree?"

"You mean your fish dying?" Layton said, trying to deflect him.

"You heard about that. Well, that and a guy shooting at me in Japan, thinking I was Horace. Then, Horace turning up dead. The

President – did he throw a chair at you that day in the Oval? The Wilderness Bill – we start in Japan, a wealthy country? "

Layton had turned icy cold now as he stared back at his questioner.

"What's your point?"

Nothing. Layton was giving up nothing. Still, David waded into deeper, more treacherous waters.

"I happened upon your briefcase in the car the other day on my way back from the Hill. I, uh, happened to look inside."

Layton's gaze remained steady.

David could feel himself growing warmer as he stammered on. 'In for a dime, in for a dollar.'

"I have been feeling lately . . . well, actually, I have been trying to put things together. Look, I know we talked about six months. I guess I just have been wondering if we were getting involved in a piece of legislation that maybe isn't what it seems to be . . . on the surface, I mean . . ."

"Go on." Layton could be an exasperating man when he chose to be.

Now David did want his drink. He took a long moment to have a gulp. No more manly drawing room smoking a cigar sips: 'Gin, help me. Help me now.'

Layton picked up the thread.

"Find anything?"

"Sir? Oh, you mean . . . well, yes and no. I mean, there was also a diplomatic pouch in Marge's desk. I guess I really went too far. Wanted you to know, is all . . . I only saw a list of Japanese towns. And a lot of money. I broke the lock, I'm afraid. A light was flashing on the pouch . . ."

"And shortly after that, your fish were killed. Right?"

David wished he knew where this was going. All he could answer was "Right."

The Secretary rose from the couch, with a nod offered David a re-fill. David declined. Layton took his time placing ice cubes in his tumbler and adding the gin. He seemed to be weighing something. To accept David's resignation on the spot?

He paced in front of David, sipping his drink as he began speaking.

"Alright then, thirty lashes for the detective work. But you will get only a 'C-minus' grade for your conclusions, whatever the hell they might be."

Layton raised a hand in warning.

"Oh, don't say, don't say. I can guess anyway. Now then. I am sorry about your fish. A terrible thing to lose one's fish."

At his feeble attempt at humor, the shoe was now on the other foot. David glared back at him.

Layton, realizing his misstep, continued in a more serious tone.

"I can only say a few things which may be helpful to your situation."

His 'situation?' What 'situation?'

"Number one, without going into the details, you are well aware that Matt Walker and I are no longer close. Not that we ever were that close to begin with. More to the point, I hope the son of a bitch drops dead tonight when he's busy screwing one of those girlfriends of his. Oh-ho! Do not quote me, understand."

"Too much water's passed under our bridge by now, no point being less than frank. Sometimes, I wonder what the hell it is, we are trying to accomplish. They keep talking about the 'greater good.' Hell, isn't that just another version of 'The ends justify the means?' So, in that regard, your instincts are probably on target."

"Now then. There is much more I will not say to you. Cannot say. For your own good. . . .

. . . 'Dear Boy.'"

How he hated that name!

"Now then. You have been loyal and a helluva legislative undersecretary. But I want you to be able to return home soon. I know the toll this has taken on you. First, however, I have a favor to ask. Let's you and me, finish up this Wilderness bill. Oh, not for the Southern Prince, you understand. For the country. Because, regardless of Walker's shenanigans, there is the greater good contained within it.

Let us do this for our country. Think of it as our legacy, yours and mine. Once we're done, we'll both high-tail it outta town, like I said before. What's that?"

David hadn't said anything.

"Nothing. I was just listening."

"Have we got ourselves a deal then? Stay on a few more months?"

David felt a mix of emotions. He was relieved by the Secretary's continued confidence. For the second time in as many weeks, he was surprised not to be fired. But mostly, he was curious as to what Layton would not say. Inquiring birds want to know. Here, in the privacy of a cabinet official's home, he had learned little more than what he knew a few hours earlier. Yet, he found himself nodding yes, trusting Layton one more time.

Signing on for the duration.

Again.

Outside, a winter's rain had begun. The drops stung his face as he walked to the waiting car. Halfway down the walk, the front door reopened, and Layton emerged waving an envelope.

"I almost forgot. Here're four tickets to Mrs. Lechman's little soiree at that new store. I bought up some extras, for a good cause and all. Her children's cancer fund. Round up some friends and come on out. Hear tell it's going to be quite the evening. Oh, yeh. And our favorite politician's going to be in attendance. Wouldn't want to miss that, now would we?"

With that, Layton slapped David on the back and ran back inside.

'Dream Girl.' He would finally meet up with 'Dream Girl.' For a while as he rode back to town, David floated on thoughts of a certain liveaboard in Seattle's harbor. Of a leggy woman with a long red braid, tanned legs in a pair of white shorts, as she swept the deck. Of his sons taking their little Sunfish for spirited sails around the harbor. Of peace, harmony. Happiness. A life. A real life.

"Ernie Fields, my ass!"

As the big car entered Georgetown's M Street, David's eyes fell on a newspaper the Secretary had left behind on the seat. The reading light cast a warm light revealing an article that had been circled. Curious, David read the headline:

"Animal Deformities Found in Montana's National Parks."

Buried deep in the article was information that several shipping containers from Japan bearing international radiation insignias had been spotted in the park by local residents. A scientist was quoted as saying the animals' deformities were consistent with radioactive poisoning.

"Holy shit."

CJ answered him. "What's that, Kelly?"

"Just something in the paper. No big deal. But, hey, CJ, is it me, or is the world getting a whole lot meaner?"

"It's not you."

"Didn't think so."

David knew. He knew damned well. Here was his quid pro quo. Japan's UniStar must have something to do with some sort of radioactive storage in his wilderness areas. That he supposedly was saving. With his law. Written by his team.

Who were these people, anyway?

When he got home, he took a long, hot shower. Wasn't that what rape victims were said to do? To wash away the assault?

Then he called the boys, heard the day's soccer scores. He realized they were what mattered. Not some random news article left in Layton's car.

Six more months.

'Dream Girl.'

Fiddle-dee-dee.

CHAPTER THIRTY-FIVE

National Institutes of Health
Bethesda, Maryland

A news conference was called by research doctors affiliated with the Lechman Children's Cancer Research Trust. Sybil, looking tanned and rested from her recent long week-end on the island, sat at the head table, wearing her trademark lavender suit. Little 'Pushkin' sat quietly in his wicker basket at her feet. Medical reporters on the 'cancer beat,' other members of the scientific media, oncology pediatricians, nurses, young patients, and family members eagerly filled the room.

They were gathered to hear exciting news. The team's new 'Magic Bullets' cell bonding therapy had been showing astounding success. The children in the program had all boasted healthy remissions in their blood cancers. Their hair was re-growing, their energy levels were returning.

Until today, the parents had dealt only with medical staff, secretaries, sad-faced counselors. Board members and the trust's president, Sybil Lechman, operated largely in the background, unseen by those most affected by their work. Up to now, they were nothing more than names on the trust fund's letterhead. Signatures on decisive letters, granting admittance and patient guidelines to those in the coveted 'last chance' research program.

No one would have associated so serious an endeavor with the woman seated at the lectern today. Ignoring those around her, she carefully applied another coat of lipstick, peering at her reflection in her jewel-encrusted compact. Her little dog whimpered, and she picked him up, holding him during the entire program, seemingly oblivious to the inappropriateness of her action. In short, the woman appeared wealthy, arrogant and out of touch.

But the parents were not judging anyone on that level today. Their heads were in the clouds as they participated in the happy news. The Trust, which had poured millions into this current research effort, had succeeded beyond their wildness hopes. They were licking childrens' cancers of the blood. No one would fault a society woman for her lavender suit and chancy behavior only a week past her husband's funeral. Certainly, no one in this room.

Near the back of the room stood a family of four – husband, wife and two sons. They were well dressed and the boys, aged eleven and thirteen, were well behaved. The man had bandages on most of his fingers. Other than that, they were a normal-appearing family. The man peered intently at the panel, listening carefully to the speeches by researchers.

Towards the end of the presentation, the program's benefactress was introduced. At the lectern, she still had ahold of 'Pushkin.' A pair of reading glasses hung on a chain – they too were lavender and bejeweled. Pointed ends of the glasses stuck out at an odd angle from her face as she began speaking from her script.

The audience knew vaguely of her society woman status and that she now represented her late husband on the Trust. Her appearance seemed to say the rest. However, when she spoke, she was eloquent and heartfelt. She told them of her late husband's humanity. Of his humble beginnings. Of his life-long good health. And of her horror at the news of his sudden death in a recent boating accident.

The woman holding the terrier went on about her commitment to ridding children of cancer, now that her husband was gone. She even went so far as to break her cardinal rule of not complaining when she revealed the loss of her son years earlier to childhood cancer.

Finally, she recited one of Horace's favorite poems, by Wendell Barry. The words spoke volumes about 'Madame Benefactress' as even hardened medical reporters, on deck for hard news, listened.

"When despair for the world grows in me and I wake in the night at the least sound in fear of what my life and my children's lives may be, I go and lie down where the wood drake rests in his beauty on the water, and the great heron feeds. I come into the peace of wild things who do not tax their lives with forethought of grief. I come into the presence of still water. And I feel above me the day-blind stars waiting with their light. For a time, I rest in the grace of the world and am free."

By the end of the reading, there was not a dry eye in the room. The big man with the sky-blue eyes and bandaged fingers found himself holding his son's hand too tightly as he struggled with his own feelings. Never before had he come so close to the consequences of his actions. Today, worlds collided, and compartmentalization failed.

"Now then," the woman concluded, "let us all move forward to enjoy active, healthy lives."

The room erupted in spontaneous applause for her as people rushed forward to press her hand. It was more than she wanted or expected, but Sybil endured it all with uncharacteristic grace. She hated sentimentality. It made her squirm. As soon as she could, she got the hell out, back to her Middleburg farm.

CHAPTER THIRTY-SIX

"Way to go, Sybil!" David thought from the comfort of his armchair.

He caught her remarks on CSPAN. He found her recitation of the Barry poem surprising. But it showed yet another side to a complicated woman. The world saw only the privilege. Yet there was so much more.

David suffered from Potomac Fever – a localized DC condition in which political junkies are addicted to rubbing elbows with powerful people in the news. Victims of the condition grow accustomed to having the inside track, to knowing the news before it happens.

As a Washington insider, David increasingly could read between the lines about his new friend. He noticed Sybil was distancing herself from the President lately. She was a no-show at a Walker fund-raiser, citing her continued grief at the death of her husband. "Bull shit," David thought. The woman, while grief-stricken, was made of iron. If she'd wanted to be there, she would have been front and center. Wild horses couldn't have kept her away.

'Dear Boy' had things about right.

Despite Jeffrey Layton's loving advice, Sybil couldn't help herself. For her, suspicion, grief and intuition had come together to form a seething, unquenchable hatred for Matthew Walker. When all was said and done, her Horace had described it all for her in his letter. Black and white. His message was unavoidable.

Her personal safety, be damned. Sybil would not be cast aside. 'The little woman.' Quietly feminine to the end. If that was what Matthew Walker thought, he was indeed mistaken. He had begun something he thought had ended at the Washington Cathedral.

"Not by a long shot," thought The Widow.

But she was strategic and wily. Keeping to Layton's well-considered advice, she called her lawyers. She played the distraught widow for them. She displayed her feminine vulnerabilities as she assured her big, strong counselors of her mistake at even suggesting any action against the President of the United States.

Of course, her important lawyers had assured her, they knew she was speaking from extreme grief. They knew she appreciated the President's friendship, all that he had done for her. All that he was to her late husband. In short, they bought Sybil's contrition hook, line and sinker.

. . . 'I would first like to thank the Academy . . .'

Not for nothing had she practiced her helpless feminine act these many years.

Yet the cat, as the saying goes, was out of the bag. Law firms in Washington, D.C., as elsewhere, leak like sieves. A partner at Lechman's law firm happened to have drinks with a White House attorney. Had happened – no names, please – to mention a certain wealthy widow who was contemplating taking legal action against the Chief Executive. Two voices became three, and soon the President was aware of Sybil's wrath.

Later, he also was made aware of her withdrawal of action. Walker noted with satisfaction the protection his office afforded. People feared him. Feared the White House. Even wealthy widows dared not approach. Ladies in lavender knew enough to steer clear. Exactly as he liked it.

He and his political crew re-counted the money. TV campaigns already were in post-production by a well-known political smear merchant in New York City. (So good that both sides used him.) The reelection campaign of Matthew Walker, "The Wilderness President," was in full swing.

However, while the threat of a lawsuit was withdrawn, drawing room action was another matter. Washington's Georgetown is a legendary incubator of national gossip. Persons of a certain stature -- and they know who they are -- regularly meet along Wisconsin Avenue, as well as "M," "N," "O," and "P" Streets to sip costly wines and issue informal report cards on current administrations.

They understand that inclusion in their set is the wish of all sitting presidents. Commanders in Chief aspire to hob-nob with newspaper publishers and wealthy patrons, whose judgements ring 'round the world in their pricey haunts -- Jackson Hole, Aspen, Gstaad, Montego Bay, Montecito. . ..the list goes on.

Somewhere in the world, at some time, someone from a Georgetown salon is talking. And a crowd is listening. Presidents know to watch carefully these rear actions. Icebergs 'neath the waters can be lethal to ships of state.

Sybil was a Georgetown matron in good standing. As such, her views were sought. She was on the inside track of the Walker Administration from the beginning. Many even considered her the "Founding Mother," working alongside her devoted partisan husband.

Together, they had served the Sera's and Chardonnay's, the brie's and pates, assuring Walker's entry to their estimable set. Paid his way. Smoothed over his flaws. Explained the unexplainable. In short, President Walker had taken a long, prosperous ride on the Lechman tab.

It all began over lunch one day. Sybil was asked her view of Walker's proposal to carve off most of Alaska for a new wilderness area. Many in her group had husbands who regarded the state as their personal playground for fishing and hunting. An entire region where men could be men without the steady drone of the female voice.

Up to that luncheon, until that moment of the passing of the crumbled Roquefort cheese for the ladies' delicate salads, Sybil had been discreet. Had kept her own counsel. Others took her silence for a widow's understandable grief. No one questioned her lack of fire about the President. Her views were well known. Her allegiance unquestioned.

Perhaps she was overly tired that day. Perhaps the chilled Chardonnay had been a bit too delicious. Because, as the ladies at lunch carefully noted, her silence took on a slight, but noticeable curling of her Elizabeth Ardened red-stained lip.

It was not so much what she said, nor even what she did not say. It was her body language as she said very little. The 'ladies who lunch' quickly picked up on the signals as effectively as a group of Kalahari Bushmen. Soon enough, the town was buzzing with rumors of Walker's loss of support from this important quarter.

Many wishing no better than to toady to the powerful Lechman cartel, joined the chorus. Soon, doubts were being quoted in the town's society columns. Unattributed remarks unfavorable to Walker began showing up in the tabloids in New York. Could serious journalistic critiques be far off?

The only answer, on the part of the Walker camp, was "No."

Such a down-tick in public opinion could develop into full-blown calamity, if left unattended. Attention had to be paid. Leon Barshevsky, keeper of the flame, broached the subject to the President one-night enroute to Russia on Air Force One. The two, as was their custom, spoke in code, but each understood what the other was saying.

Barshevsky began over drinks.

"Mr. President, you have, I take it, had the opportunity to note yesterday's Post Style Section about that Lechman luncheon last week?"

Matt Walker did not answer. Instead, he ignored Barshevsky much as a petulant child about to be punished might. But it was late, there was nowhere to run, and the Schnauzer was determined.

Again, he spoke.

"This cannot continue. We know where it will lead. We dare not have such negative items in the news, particularly from this quarter. I can take care of this for you, if you will allow it."

"Leon, you are overly worried, as usual. And your solutions, which I am coming to learn, are overly harsh. Let it go."

At the ultimatum, Barshevsky crossed the small cabin area, and handed Walker an envelope labeled Lechman Industrial Bank of New York. "This may serve to change your mind."

The President took the envelope, removed a ten-page letter and read it in its entirety. As Sybil and Jeffrey had done before him, he carefully re-read the letter.

"Incoherent ramblings of an old man."

"Still, the widow appears to be taking it seriously enough. These luncheons of hers appear to be focused at your defeat. Very grave, in my view."

"What do you suggest? Careful now." Walker indicated with a gesture the hidden microphones they both knew were set on 'Record.'

"I have a representative who might be willing to pay her a little visit. Discuss with her the importance of the campaign. Of our issues. Enlist her support in a direct way. That is all."

"A simple meeting?"

"That is all."

"Not overly harsh?"

"Not at all, sir."

Walker weakened. Leon was right, as usual. They had come too far now to turn back. To allow this woman . . . they had saved too much land from the corporate raiders. Had built too fine a presidential record. Four more years, the Alaska bill, and his legacy as the "Wilderness President" would be assured.

Leon's suggestion would keep his reputation on track with the ladies who lunch. Ladies whose influence over American politics was immeasurable. The old men died, leaving them the wealth. The ladies chose causes and political leaders to support. They moved their dollars around at will among pet causes. Walker was in line for many of those dollars. Leon's plan would ensure no break in their largesse.

Glancing at the cameras overhead in the plane's cabin, Walker gave an imperceptible nod of the head. Leon noted it. Message received. Proposal approved. There had been no paperwork. No aides. No committee reports. Not so much as a call to the head of the party.

Some matters could be handled more expeditiously.

Gabby widows were in that category.

CHAPTER THIRTY-SEVEN

It was a night for surprises. One minute, David was clearing away his dishes from dinner, with an excellent new murder mystery awaiting his attention at his armchair by the fireplace. The next, his phone was ringing, and someone was at his front door.

As he removed his phone from its cradle, there was a pause and click, as everyone came on the line. Finally, he heard Sybil's voice. Walking with the phone to the door, he was surprised to see Monica standing in the hallway, with her suitcase. A new camera installed by his 'fish marauders' took note of his surprise. He waved Monica in, indicating he was on the phone.

Stepping behind the kitchen door, he recognized Sybil's voice, halfway through her opening sentence.

" . . simply am so distraught lately. David? Are you there?"

"Uh, yes. Yes, I'm listening. Distraught, you say?"

" . . that I was wondering, and of course, you are under no obligation to . . ."

Monica edged into the kitchen. "Okay if I leave my suitcase over here?"

"David? I can hear that you have someone there . . . I am so sorry to have called you at such an hour . . ."

"No, Sybil. Listen, it is fine. Actually, more than fine. I have been wanting to speak to you as well."

. . . to learn the identity of 'Dream Girl,' he thought . . .

" . .. this can wait . . ."

"No, no. Please. How may I help?"

"Alright then. I am having a few guests to the Farm this week-end. Could you join us? I really do need a special friend."

. . . what about Jeffrey? he thought.

Instead, he said, "Will there be the same people as at Montego Bay?"

There. He asked his question. In front of Monica. In front of this lovely woman, he was conniving to meet 'Dream Girl.' What a jerk!

The Widow didn't get it. Her answer was self-absorbed.

"Yes, possibly, plus a few others besides. Oh, David. Thank you so very much. I have pressing matters to discuss. And I have a feeling you may be just the person who might help me to sort things out."

... me? What about Jeffrey? David thought. But the date was made and soon enough, he turned to deal with the gorgeous blonde soap opera actress standing in the middle of his Carmel-style kitchen who was removing her scarf.

Monica's spontaneous visit was troubling. Their relationship, if you could call it that, had not progressed to this stage. At least in David's mind. But his resolve melted away as his intruder helped herself to a glass of his wine. In the same manner as Sybil, Monica seemed to take over the space. The woman was here. Life takes a holiday.

He made her one of his gourmet omelets and heard all of her news about her sudden fame and a television movie she was doing. She bubbled over with happiness at her good fortune as she poked around his kitchen, admiring his copper cooking ware. Soon enough, the proprietor of the establishment invited his guest to the bedroom.

As before, however, there was no passion. Only discomfort and guilt on David's part. He imagined 'Dream Girl' at inappropriate moments. Again, David felt nothing. No need was met. He rose early as Monica slept. She was a beautiful woman, he noted. Peaches and cream complexion. Sweet disposition.

"What the hell more could a man want?" he asked himself.

He made breakfast. Tons of fresh coffee. The smells woke her. Wearing one of his shirts, Monica wandered into the kitchen. David waited until they had eaten and were seated by the fireplace before he spoke.

"Monica. You are such a terrific person. Talented. Beautiful. And a wonderful companion. But the truth is, I will be heading back to the Pacific Northwest soon. I will be resuming my life there with my two sons. I have an ex-wife. I have a career to restart out there. You, on the other hand, are just taking off. 'The Gathering Storm,' I presume is not the highest you will go. You are already in a feature TV film. Hell, someday I will be paying money at some theater in Seattle to see you on the big screen."

There. He had said it. And rather well, he thought. Nothing personal. Just the facts. Interspersed with a few well-placed compliments. The lobbyist at work . . . in his personal life . . .

Monica received his words cautiously. She could not disagree with any of it. Except, perhaps, the bit about leaving the East Coast. Who left the East Coast? Why waste one's time out west? What did they have there, fir trees? Certainly, no culture. No Metropolitan Museum. No Elaine's. No Sak's Fifth Avenue.

The two continued talking until David had to leave for work. He arranged for a special VIP pass for a tour of the White House for her. On his way out the door, his eyes fell on the gala store opening tickets sitting on the counter. Impulsively, he handed her one. Told her President Walker would be attending, along with many members of Congress.

"Congress?! The President?!"

There. David realized he had just taken decisive first steps towards re-shaping his new life. He had admitted out loud that he was leaving Washington and political life. He also managed to extricate himself from any future with Monica.

He asked only one favor about the invitation.

"Please do not wear black. That's what Walker's girlfriends all wear around him. It's kind of a town joke. So, unless you want to be taken for one of the President's women, something more colorful would be a good idea."

His invitation had the desired effect, deflecting what he felt was a 'break-up,' until he was in his elevator headed for the street.

"Great job, lover boy," he thought. He had just invited a 'date' to his evening with 'Dream Girl.' What an idiot. Strategic life management? Not a chance!

And once again, he had mis-read the actress.

"... So, unless you want to be taken for one of the President's women, something more colorful would be a good idea."

Monica nodded as she contemplated the delicious possibility. Already, she had in mind a certain black Armani gown . . .

CHAPTER THIRTY-EIGHT

Upon his return from Russia, Leon made a call. To the basement office near the White House. Uncharacteristically, he wanted to meet with his representative in person this time. The man with bandaged fingers showed up promptly for his assignment.

He was to travel to the Lechman Estate in Middleburg. He was to have a little talk with Madam Lechman. Barshevsky even provided him with a script. There were to be no deviations. He was to see the woman, scare the pants off her, deliver the speech, then get the hell out. Were there any questions? The man had none. Save the quaking feeling in his ankles that suddenly appeared. Otherwise, the Presidential Schnauzer had been clear about his mission. Crystal clear.

One last thing: He was to implement the plan as soon as possible.

CHAPTER THIRTY-NINE

David found himself looking forward to his weekend in Middleburg. Great food, a heated swimming pool, and Sybil always seemed to have interesting guests. Maybe even 'Dream Girl' this time?

He was disappointed to learn the guest roster consisted of several Fortune 500 couples, wealthy, older, pleasant, but unexciting. She seemed to be going for an easy week-end. Nothing too stimulating. Layton was there and seemed more relaxed around David. Clearly, he and his boss had grown closer. They were co-conspirators of a sort, although David remained unclear exactly about what.

As usual, David was left on his own, to swim, take hikes, play tennis. His presence, as in Montego Bay, was only commanded for the formal dinner in the mansion's glass enclosed atrium. Oriental rugs, potted palms, gins and tonics. Another swell evening. Frank Sinatra played softly in the background. Again, Layton and Sybil were nose-to-nose.

Coffee and pastries on the terrace. People drifting off. Sybil and Jeffrey once again closeted. Just as David was preparing to make his way back to his room, Sybil showed up, alone.

"Now then. My dear. Thank you so much for joining us. Such a comfort."

David could tell. This was it. Whatever the hell 'it' was. He made polite chit-chat as he prepared himself.

"Do you want to know something funny?"

As usual, Sybil did not await response but engineered ahead. David was just as glad to let her talk.

"We have, Horace and myself, this friend. He enjoys the occasional Cuban cigar with my Horace. From Horace's personal supply. Well, he asked me the other day if my Horace had been a Communist? . . . can you imagine such a thing? Because of his cigars, you see. The man assumed Horace was a confidante of Fidel. Isn't that just too amusing?"

"I assure you my Horace was no Communist. A patriot. American patriot. Through and through. And what if he became disappointed in his country? What then? Who might he have angered?"

David couldn't tell if he should answer. So far, things seemed rhetorical.

"Ma'am. I think, although I was never privileged to know your husband, that his reputation is beyond reproach. Why, it is well known that President Walker owes his presidency to your husband's efforts."

"Exactly. And that is my point."

What point? David was growing unsteady . . .

"What if a son betrays a father? What then?"

What to answer?

"Where can the wife turn? Who will recompense her? I ask you."

What the devil?

"How severe should retribution be? How close to home? At what level does one take risks to avenge a death?

Now David could guess. Suddenly, he no longer wanted to be here. "You think the storm was . . ."

" . . was not the cause, let us say . . ."

Crap! Socializing at this level was getting way too dangerous. Where was this all heading?

Abruptly, Sybil walked over to him. She gave him a loving hug and a peck on the cheek. "Thank you. I'm glad we had this little chat. I believe I am clear now."

With her strange words, Sybil left the patio, leaving David to make his own way back to the down coverlets and thousand-count French sheets. Ah, luxury, he thought as he sank back.

Before he slept, he considered Sybil. Layton. Monica. The President. The Wilderness Bill. A certain Seattle anchorage. Two freckle-face boys. And 'Dream Girl.' As usual, he knew nothing. And was in a total state of confusion.

Better that way. Better not to know . . .

CHAPTER FORTY

As ordered, the assassin went to work. He researched Madam Lechman's schedule, learning when she was likely to be at home on the estate. Sybil was peripatetic, so his research was difficult. Eventually, he learned that on one day in fourteen, the farm's stablemen were the only ones on duty.

He determined the closest date, circled it on a calendar he kept in his wallet. Then the man did something he had never done before. He joined his wife and children in church. He prayed to God. He silently asked for help. Of all the jobs he had been asked to do in his long and checkered career, this was the worst.

The day of the mission arrived bright and sunny.
Frank drove his car out Rt. 50 about 45 miles west of Washington until he reached Virginia Hunt Country. He passed by old Rt. 29-211, now a freeway. He passed the former location of a diner that until recently had proudly refused service to blacks.

What a strange country, he thought. Stranger still, the task at hand. Frank, to his friends, was not into harming women. Under normal circumstances, he would have refused the job. Unbeknownst to the Schnauzer, however, this particular operative actually welcomed the opportunity to visit 'chez Lechman.'

He stopped in the toney village of Middleburg for an egg salad sandwich and fresh lemonade. No frozen juices here. This was Middleburg. A parallel universe. He noticed a distinct air of ease on Main Street. No one was in a hurry. No one needed to be anywhere. Everyone had chilled martinis waiting at home.

The man made no attempt to hide. Clean-cut, he blended right in. They probably took him for a polo player. Weren't they very fit as well? Frank, to his friends, even drove the family car with its own Virginia plates. No subterfuge this day. Because he had long since determined that his mission today was not Leon Barshevsky's. Not by a long shot.

Make no mistake, Frank was on shaky ground. He had no idea what the widow's reactions would be But he knew what he had to do. And that knowledge was delivering a peace and comfort he had not felt in many years.

His tires crunched on the tiny gravel that seemed to distinguish wealthy driveways the world over. He was unsurprised when Sybil herself answered the door.

"Yes?"

"I cannot tell you my name. But I am employed by the President. He has sent me here with a message for you. May I come in ma'am?"

"I am not in the habit of admitting strangers with no appointment. Representing the president, you say? The president of what?"

"Matthew Walker, ma'am."

"Just a moment then."

Sybil abruptly closed the door, clicking the dead-bolt lock into place. Two minutes later, she returned. As she opened the door wide, he could see that she had a revolver aimed dead at him. Smart lady.

"Yes, ma'am. And I assume you know how to shoot that gun?"

"Want to take a chance and find out?"

"No. No. I believe that you must do this for protection. I can assure you, however, that I mean you no harm. Quite the opposite, as a matter of fact. Please, may I have a moment of your time?"

Sybil was nothing if now curious. Who was this odd man, claiming to represent Matthew? Well, the gun was loaded, and she was a crack shot. So, she ushered him into her sunroom. There, he took a seat in an antique lady's sewing rocker. He was a large man and she found him a bit comical seated thus with his long legs tucked up under his chest.

He appeared much less threatening than when he stood before her at the front door. She relaxed a little but kept her grip on the gun. Lest this man was newly escaped from God knows where. One could take no chances these days. No appointment. No name. On her help's day off. With a grandiose claim of representing the President.

Well, she'd as soon shoot him as not. The sheriff would visit, take away the body. Her help could clean up the blood. She noted with satisfaction the tiled floor in the sunroom. No rugs would be ruined.

"Begin," she ordered.

"I don't suppose you would recognize me. I was one of the parents at your N.I.H. news conference the other day. About curing rare childhood cancers of the blood. My son, Quinn, is enrolled in your generous program. Doing much better as a matter of fact. Due to you and your husband's good will."

"Well, why didn't you say so in the first place? Why all this silly nonsense about Matt Walker?"

Frank, to his friends, took a deep breath. Here goes. Bombs away!

"Because there is much, much more. What I have to say will shock you and it will sadden you. I am so sorry about all this. . . Mrs. Lechman, I would prefer to speak without that gun aimed at me . . . here, allow me to move my chair back a few feet, for your peace of mind while I say what I need to say . . ."

"First, please take this and read it."

The man extended his hand with the Barshevsky script. Sybil read it and looked up at him, more puzzled than ever.

"I must say, Mr., whatever your name is, now I am completely confused. You have me at a disadvantage, I am afraid."

The man lowered his voice and slowly told her his story. He told her of his true profession. At this information, gently delivered, Sybil again aimed the gun at the man's head. He continued talking. He told her of the special team that reported to Leon Barshevsky. He told her some of their past activities.

Finally, he gave her the grim details of her husband's death. At this point, he played her a tape of Walker's final words to Horace. The widow's gun hand began shaking uncontrollably while her other hand grabbed at her blouse. She appeared too upset to cry. She waited to hear every last detail.

When the man finished, she whispered, "Why? Why do you come here now to tell me such a story? What kind of a monster are you?"

He reminded her of his assignment. To come here, to speak the words on the piece of paper, to place a long hunting knife to her throat. To promise a return visit, or worse, a visit to her loved ones, should she fail to comply with Walker's request.

She would cease all active opposition to Walker's reelection efforts. The only thing Walker left her was her vote. She was welcome to vote against him – no threats covered that action.

Now the man began to cry. He had killed her husband. Her husband had saved his son. It was an unbalanced equation. He was here to right it in any way he could. To confess to her. To bring her the truth, whatever the cost. To prostrate himself before her. To beg her forgiveness.

There was a very long silence. Suddenly, the gun slipped from Sybil's grasp, her fist uncurled, and Madam slumped unconscious onto the clean Spanish tile floor. The man rushed to her side. Placed her on a couch. He made his way to the kitchen for water. He used the smelling salts he had brought to revive her. He had expected this or worse, after all.

As Sybil came around, her eyes were cloudy. As she refocused them, he was in the frame. Large, blue eyes, she noticed. Taut jawline. Muscular. A killer, after all. Murderer. Assassin.

As it happened, the two picked back up on their conversation. In due course, Sybil wandered into the kitchen and heated them both up some beef stew. They had a few glasses of wine. Alright, more than a few.

"What would my Horace think?" she thought. "Sitting here, serving dinner to his killer."

How truly odd the world was. By the end of the man's visit, they had discussed many things. Before leaving her, the killer left her the tape in case of any future threats. In return, she agreed to maintain the fiction that something had redirected her political support back to Matt Walker.

That was their story. When he arrived, he was a stranger. When he finally aimed the family car down the farm's long, tree-lined drive, he was a partner.

An accomplice.

Because no one crossed Sybil Lechman.

Not even the President.

CHAPTER FORTY-ONE

"Nobody can be exactly like me. Even I have trouble doing it."
Tallulah Bankhead

Le Bagatelle's was buzzing -- a week away from the opening night gala, but just minutes until a mid-week customers' preview evening. David, never a shopper, found himself standing shoulder to shoulder with 'Ladies Who Lunch' outside the chic new store in Chevy Chase, Maryland, waiting to be admitted.

On the prowl.

For 'Dream Girl.'

He felt like an excited teenager as he searched the open atrium for her. Several times, he followed women with auburn hair, but each time, he was mistaken. He paced throughout the grand four-story structure that was divided not so much by floors, as by atmospherics. A waterfall cascaded down the four levels, giving the store a relaxing sound. Gorgeous models paraded about in the latest designer creations. Sparkling champagne was served from silver trays to patrons.

Frustrated, he finally asked a guard about her. He described her long braid. And a leg cast she might still be wearing.

"Oh, you mean Lexi. Leslie Cameron. Yeh, I know her. Well, I tell you, everything you see tonight, I'm saying everything, was her idea. What a woman!"

"It's all outstanding. Can you tell me where I might find her to offer my congratulations?"

"Home, man. You would find her home. She was up all night with last-minute things, poor baby. So we sent her home to crash. But hey! You coming to the gala? She'll be here for that. Sure enough!"

What the guard didn't share was a fight that took place earlier involving 'Dream Girl' and America's finest, the United States Secret Service. While she worked to accommodate the men's intense security needs, tension built as they seemed to take over her event. They needed special locks to storerooms. Building plans. Cameras placed in places the store had not planned.

They reviewed the gala guest list, running everyone's Social Security numbers through a rigorous database.

Finally, the men were found pawing through Designer Rudolpho's priceless gowns with hands that moments earlier sifted the fine dirt in the atrium's large potted plants. Rudolpho went ballistic as

'Planet Hollywood' met the 'Marine Code.' Secret Service or no Secret Service, he was having none of it.

"Here now! What the hell do you think you are doing?"

"We have to check, sir. All part of procedures."

"I'll tell you where you can put your procedures!"

At this, the officers in unison took a step closer to the designer, hands nearing their weapons. Rudi, realizing his mistake, backed off with a nervous giggle.

"Hey fellas. Listen. We all have a job to do here. I am Rudolpho, the store's opening night designer. Perhaps you have heard of me. Whatever you need, man. I'm here for you. The nation's business. Yes. All the way, Jose. Swish, swish, I'm here."

'Dream Girl,' sensing trouble approached.

"Gentlemen. Is everything alright here?"

The lead agent spoke. "We are beginning our inspection now as your shipments arrive. There will be a team of dogs on site shortly."

Again, Rudi erupted.

"Dogs?! Did he say 'dogs'? These are priceless creations. I simply cannot allow slobbering mutts . . ."

Once more the agents circled the designer. Once again, Rudi realized the error of his ways.

"Dogs are good. I like dogs myself. Have two of my own. Hey, I think the President's great. I didn't vote for him. But I could have. I mean, only two choices there. What are 'ya going to do?"

In summary, this had been 'Dream Girl's' life lately. Refereeing crazy fashionistas as they encountered strait-laced men in suits. Different agendas. Different perspectives. Very nearly, different worlds.

Finally, she had had enough of troubling linear beings from Washington. And had retired to the safety of her apartment.

Missing her third appointment with 'Dear Boy.'

There was always the gala.

CHAPTER FORTY-TWO

Bluntly put, Sybil was an atheist. Over the years, she had softened her story, saying simply that she did not know. But that was not so. She knew. She knew damned well that here was all there was. Make the best of it and move on. This is not to say the woman lacked a moral compass. Far from it. She was at heart a good woman who had, on balance, done more good than harm during her lifetime.

Lately, however, as guardian of 'the secrets,' she was engaged in some heavy-duty thinking. She found herself falling deeper and deeper into a desire for revenge based on her honest belief that a wicked man was at the country's helm.

She did her best thinking in Montego Bay. So, while others clasped their hymnals close to their breasts, mourning lost loved ones, Sybil walked the white sandy beaches near her home, letting her mind wander over events of the past few months, and what she would do.

She had already committed to a certain course of action. Therefore, her musings were her way of verifying her thought processes, so dire were her conclusions. Finally, The Widow returned to Washington fully comfortable. She had weighed her options. She had examined her thinking. Now, she needed to make a few important calls.

Her first call was to Stan McIntyre, her personal accountant from many years back, before her wealthy marriages required teams of bean counters to keep track of the wealth. They had not spoken for years, and he was surprised to hear from her. He was even more surprised when he learned of her wish to hire him to do some work.

Sybil needed to be her own person. She required absolute confidentiality. She knew that Lechman International's accountants were in bed with Lechman International's attorneys, and God knew who else. The corporate ciphers were useful in corporate matters.

For her present course, however, Stan was a trusted advisor. With his able and discreet assistance, she was able to move some funds around in such a way as to cause no undue notice. These funds – a considerable amount – were reposted offshore for The Widow's special needs.

Next up, she called Leslie Cameron at Le Bagatelle's about the invitee list to the opening gala. Under a tight deadline imposed by the Secret Service, all names had been provided, along with Social Security numbers, so that the service could check guests' credentials. Sybil already had submitted her list of names weeks earlier.

Now, she wanted to add names and would purchase an extra dinner table for her additional guests. Interestingly, two of her last-minute guests were blind. One was an attorney at the Department of Justice, someone Sybil had known for years. The lawyer's special guest would be an aide to a famous West Coast mayor. Their contact information was carefully logged for agent follow-up. The more, the merrier. All was in order.

Next, the Widow Lechman went shopping. She bought a new party dress in New York. It was long, lavender, and featured an elegant portrait neckline that would show off her jewels to advantage. She also stopped into a stereo shop. She needed to purchase some recording equipment. Normally, she would allow others to perform such menial shopping tasks. But this once, she wanted to check the items personally.

She had embarked on her mission. There would be no mistakes. There would be no security lapses. Horace would be pleased.

Sybil's 'partner' also was busy making preparations of his own. He too needed special equipment. But his shopping venues were more circumspect than Sybil's. His 'products' were purchased in dark alleys overseas using unmarked cars. His 'products' were not available on the open market. You pretty much had to know someone to shop.

The man was dealing in chemicals, right-of-entry papers, forged identities. The stuff of the underworld. He had traversed this world continuously throughout his long career, on behalf of others and their causes. This time, he was traversing for himself. He would guard his family, resurrect his soul, pay overdue debts.

Not a bad mission, one that, on balance, was far more honorable than previous activities. One thing for sure, this would be his first job requiring a tuxedo. Accordingly, one of his stops was to a recommended tailor in London who stitched for him one of the finest tuxedos, money could buy. When one is committing murder in high society, after all, one must be impeccably turned out.

Also shopping for formal wear was a bevy of attractive blondes stretching from New York to North Carolina. All but one was a presidential girlfriend. All but one had been told by the President how well their blonde tresses and tanned skins looked against black.

All but one planned to get lucky at the party. Planned an evening at the Washington Hotel with the Chief Executive. All but one had concocted stories for their husbands or boyfriends outlandish enough to buy them the needed time for intimacy with Matt Walker. In short, if selected, they chose to serve.

In the meantime, Monica was busy hatching her own little plot. David had warned her not to wear black or risk being mistaken for a presidential mistress. He actually told the actress this piece of information with a straight face. Obviously, he knew little about show business. Because what Monica heard was "If you want to have your picture plastered all over the papers with the President, if you want people to think you're his girl, wear black to the party."

Monica had sniffed the catnip. And now was on the prowl .. for a drop-dead black frock.

CHAPTER FORTY-THREE

Showtime.

Fortunate people all over town were preparing for Le Bagatelle's gala night. The hype leading up to the event had been over the top. And members of Washington's elite 'A List' were in local spas and salons being poked and primped in hopes of being 'the fairest of them all.'

Partygoer, David Kelly, had arranged for his 'date' to stay in a hotel near Foggy Bottom. Monica arrived all aflutter. David normally avoided these kinds of events like the plague. With his freshly cleaned tuxedo hanging in the closet, he found himself anticipating the evening with mixed emotions. On the one hand, Monica was not 'the one.' She knew it. He knew it. Tonight, was little more than a 'break-up date' for both of them.

More importantly, tonight David's fantasy-land would finally meet reality. 'Dream Girl,' would occupy the same space, breath the same air. More than likely, would be preoccupied with her event. Would not remember him from that day in the park. Would see him with Monica and think, 'What an attractive couple.'

Wrong! Error! Foul. No score.

Monica was impressed with the accommodations David had arranged for her. He had booked her into the elegant Four Seasons Hotel in Georgetown. On checking in, she already had spied a major film star and a gaggle of famous super models, also in town for the opening.

In her room, she carefully removed her gown from its garment bag. She had settled on a black satin strapless sheath with bright fuchsia cummerbund. In a nod to David's warning, the dress had a matching satin evening coat, all in fuchsia with rhinestone buttons. Her hair had been re-highlighted, and a recent stay at a health spa had provided her with a fresh tan and tight abs. Working like a dog had paid off.

Tonight, she would dance with the President of the United States.

That was her plan.

Secretary Jeffrey Layton and Nellie Layton were accustomed to black tie events. After all, attendance at such events was part of the job description for cabinet members. In this work-driven town, parties were but extensions of the office. These venues provided the necessary alcohol to seal deals, grease wheels, and make moves. The Layton's attended so many soirees, in fact, that Layton had four tuxes at the ready.

Because this was Sybil's affair, Layton took particular care dressing this evening. He had every intention of being the next man in her life. Nellie, he knew, was very nearly history, but for the announcement, the recriminations and the lawyers. He had waited until his Washington term was nearly over to begin to think of ending his marriage. Cabinet members know better than to initiate messy divorce actions during mid-term elections. But now, Layton realized his time in service to his country was nearly over.

Also, another fact made its way into his thinking.

He no longer gave a 'tinker's damn' about the President's reelection chances.

So, Jeffrey Layton would make his move tonight. Sybil would have him as her life-long escort if he had his way. He loved the woman. He loved being bossed by her. He loved her wit, her intelligence, and her lavender scent as she leaned into him. He loved the way she bumped up against him accidentally on purpose.

Horace was gone now. There was no one standing in his way. Not even "The Southern Prince" could stop him. Who the hell cared about him anymore?

With Nellie's guarded acquiescence, the Layton's showed up in Middleburg to escort The Widow to her event. The Secretary went inside to collect his lady, as Nellie waited alone, as usual, in the Town Car.

Lately, Layton had noticed Sybil acting strangely. At first he chalked it up to grief, but her agitation seemed to be increasing. She was jumpy and forgetful. Maybe he ought to have her see someone. In the meantime, he offered her a Valium, and she gratefully accepted it, downing it with a cocktail. Her acceptance of chemical assistance was, in itself, a cry for help. Normally, she would have refused, and followed up her refusal with a strict, puritanical lecture about the horrors of drug dependency.

Earlier, Sybil was so upset she needed help dressing. Never before had she embarked on such an evening. Before Layton arrived, gazing at Horace's portrait, she drank down two glasses of champagne. Her gown fit her slim figure like a glove, and she withstood her drinks with no discernible difference in demeanor. The woman held her liquor well, another of her attributes.

She heard the car drive up. A fire was lit in her library. The combination of the champagne and fire warmed her, steeled her in her resolve. She clasped her bosom, letting out a short unintelligible sound and withdrew from her bodice Horace's letter. She held it close, brushed her cheek with it. Finally, she kissed the envelope and cast it into the fireplace.

"'Till death do us part, my Horace. 'Till death do us part," she said softly.

Meanwhile, over at the Four Seasons, New York's famous three "Baby Models" of tabloid fame arrived at the designer, Rudolpho's room. While hotels customarily never give out room numbers, somehow (long legs in fishnet stockings and stiletto heels?), the spirited girls were able to breach hotel security.

Pretending to be room service, and carrying an open bottle of champagne and stemware, they took over his room. The designer, taken unawares, was half-dressed. With a model's little Yorkie dancing in circles around them, the girls had their way with the openly gay man.

"Ah, come on! You've seen us naked, Rudi! Don't be shy, darling!"

Downstairs, near the elegant entrance, Monica waited for David to arrive. Suddenly, there was a commotion in the lobby. Cameras flashed. Reporters appeared from behind potted palms. Towards the entrance danced the world's most famous supermodels, dubbed "The

Baby Models" for their youth and tiny waists. They dragged a retinue of helpers and hangers on, as well as the hapless designer.

Monica felt herself being pushed back by the frantic wave of bare-legged beauty. She was unaccustomed to playing second fiddle to anyone in the looks department. But these youngsters were flying high. No one in Washington had ever seen their kind before. The store limousine arrived, and the group piled inside. One of the girls snagged the cap off a surprised bellman, planting him with a kiss on her way past.

As the car drove off, its windows lowered. Men up and down M Street smiled appreciatively as flashes of red toenails, pairs of shapely legs, ankle jewelry, seven-inch heels, and fishnet hose poked their way out of the car windows.

The girls were off to Le Bagatelle's in a cloud of giggles.

The show was about to begin.

CHAPTER FORTY-FOUR

'Break-up daters,' David and Monica soon learned the grand opening of Le Bagatelle's was divided into three parts. The gala evening kicked off with a cocktail reception in the store's elegant foyer. Drinks were followed by a seated dinner in a lavishly appointed white-tented 'casbah' set in the store's parking area.

Following dinner, there was a charity auction of Rudolpho-designed fashions modeled throughout the evening, for the benefit of the Lechman Children's Trust. Strolling musicians entertained in every part of the impressive new store and a fireworks display finished off the celebrations.

Monica's head spun as she recognized one important person after another, people she usually only glimpsed on TV. Once her fuchsia evening coat came off, she knew, the President would take special note of her enviable figure. Would take her in his arms. On-lookers, and First Lady, be damned. He would take Monica to places she never dreamed of going. Or so went the scenario to her own personal script.

While other guests arrived, everything appeared in order. As at all big events, however, behind the scenes there were other matters. Ice sculptures melted prematurely, caterers brought the wrong warming units for the casseroles, tempers flared among the staff, several models were already tipsy. All in all, a fairly typical back-stage scene, given the size and importance of the event.

Earlier, store officials needed to intercede between the pyrotechnics man and the fire marshal. Something about ammunition being set off too close to a residential area. After careful re-checking of the code, however, it was discovered that the store's commercial easement was just barely within the standard.

The technician was allowed to return to his intricate set-ups. This was the same man who staged the annual Fourth of July celebration on Washington's Mall for the nation's enjoyment each year. He knew what he was doing. He was safe-minded. He was provided an exact schedule for the timing of his starry display.

The Washington crowd, David included, thought nothing of passing through metal detectors at the entrance. They were the expected final security check for those about to party with the President. All party-goers, no matter how moneyed, no matter how elegantly attired, passed through the devices under the watchful eyes of the U.S. Secret Service.

Each guest was checked in against a roster, then issued a small lapel button to wear, indicating the level of security allowed them.

Levels were indicated by the color of one's button. While Walker regularly breached these security-imposed perimeters of safety, the measures were taken nevertheless.

It was the Service's job to ensure the President's safety despite circumstances or his mood. One glance at a guest bearing down on the Commander in Chief wearing a limited-access badge, and guards moved in, the better to react at a moment's notice in case of trouble.

Monica was pleased that she and David received the highest level of security. As an aide to a cabinet member, David's security credentials and those of his guest were unquestioned. They were low on Security's list of potential terrorists and assassins this evening.

The actress was both troubled and thrilled by all the security. Perhaps the guests, including Monica, were nothing more than bit players in Hollywood's latest high-budget action film. Maybe life was imitating art. If that were so, Monica was comfortable enough with the theatrics, given her profession. She calmly noted the armed snipers patrolling neighboring rooftops. The plain-clothed detail, however, escaped her notice. As did the real bullets loaded into officers' weapons. And Delta Force pre-positioned nearby.

The Washingtonians were used to entering buildings with guns trained on them. Thanks to the Office of Homeland Security, Navy

Seals in full combat gear were a common, ordinary sight in this official city. As common as the roving helicopters, the phalanxes of motorcycle cops, the mounted horse patrols, and bullet proof SUV's racing at high speeds on city streets, sirens blaring.

All the measures combined to make a unique security cocktail served up in the nation's capital daily in these terrorist times. For locals, the rising level of security measures no longer was noticed.

Everyone was considered suspect until proven innocent in this city on the Potomac.

In America.

Where freedom rings.

CHAPTER FORTY-FIVE

"Some enchanted evening, you may see a stranger. You may see a stranger across a crowded room, and somehow you know. You know even then, that somewhere you'll see her again and again . . ."

David was beside himself with anticipation. His eyes searched the crowd for her. Auburn hair. Slim as a willow branch. Suddenly, there she was. Across the crowded room. Monica, with her own home-grown fan club, was off to the side, laughing it up with some senators and their wives.

This was his chance. He moved through the throng, wondering as he approached her what he would say. *"Some enchanted evening, someone may be laughing. You may hear her laughing across a crowded room . . ."* He was closer now. Her auburn hair gleamed in the crystal lights . . .then she turned toward him, welcoming him into the conversational group. Not 'Dream Girl.' Not her. Another woman. Not her. Not yet.

Sybil's guests arrived two by two. Most knew each other. That included her two blind guests. They had been Washington fixtures for years and were elegant reminders that handicaps need not be handicaps.

They were bright, attractive, and fully engaged in attending one of the year's best parties as Sybil's special guests.

Their male attendant helped position them at the metal detectors. As they passed through, officers went a little numb, as do many able-bodied people when close to those with disabilities. Did they imagine themselves in that situation? Would they be able to cope as well? They momentarily shuddered at the idea of having a key part of their bodies incapacitated.

With these distracting and troubling thoughts, the guards instinctively looked away. As they did, the couple's attendant coolly passed under the agents' noses without I.D., without the inconvenience of the detector's scan, without any level of notice at all. The man's evening attire was suitably elegant. His tuxedo looked expensive, and he was quite a handsome man.

He recently had cut off his curly red hair to a Marine-style close cut. He had grown a beard that was close-trimmed and colored a light brown to match his newly colored hair. His usual cobalt blue eyes were on this night brownish black, thanks to the contact lenses he was wearing. One would fault only one item in his overall appearance. His hands were a mess. He should have taken the extra time for a manicure.

But what did it matter? He was, after all, merely a paid escort. No one would notice him. Certainly not the distracted Secret Service men as he smoothly reached out for the blind woman's arm.

"What a lovely man," cooed one society matron to another. "So very thoughtful," her friend answered.

Despite the Valium, Sybil was still acting strangely, Layton thought. Normally a gregarious, social woman who knew everyone in town, tonight Sybil was, for want of a better word, 'lurking' in the shadows. He found her standing underneath a potted palm near the entrance. She appeared to be shivering.

He stood with her as she began to interact with people. He noticed that she kept glancing nervously at the arrivals. Finally, as her blind friends arrived, she rushed excitedly over to them.

"Richard. Patty. So glad you could make it this evening." As she talked with them, she watched the attendant carefully. She addressed him: "Is everything alright then? Have you found your way?"

The attendant answered. "Yes, ma'am. I believe we all are doing very well. All is in order."

With those words, the trio edged their way into the growing crowd.

There she was. This time it really was her. Dressed in a figure-hugging dark green sheath. Her hair was piled atop her head and a tiny rhinestone clip held a few side wisps of hair in place. *". . and night after night, as strange as it seems, the sound of her laughter will sing in your dreams . . . who can explain it, who can tell you why. Fools give you reasons . . ."*

David watched as his bride gave the signal to the Marine Band to begin playing her guests into dinner. As David moved closer to the woman, he felt Monica's arm slip cozily into his. The crowd surged forward. The band played a rousing military march. And David and Monica made their way to their seats in the candle-lit tent.

Inside the tent, heaters removed the chill of a Spring evening. Candles, twinkle lights, tall trees, giant bouquets of white roses, white linens, china and silver – all accompanied the finest in wines and cuisine. Content, tanned faces fairly glowed in the elegance of the setting. The women were beautiful. The jewelry gleamed. And pre-dinner drinks ensured that diners were well on their way to experiencing a special evening as they began the second part of the evening.

Seated at the head table were the store president, Sybil, and her trustee president. Jeffrey Layton had not yet spoken to his lady. She had been busy talking with others and had seemed oddly distracted whenever he approached. He could wait until later in the evening, he thought.

"Let her see me with the missus during dinner. Give her a bit of distance."

The politician in Layton could not resist 'playing' Sybil as he did others. Goodness knows, he possessed the necessary chameleon skills. At this point in his career, charm, cunning and strategy were second nature to the Secretary. No, he would bide his time.

Once everyone was seated, there was a long silence as diners waited for the most important guests to arrive. As the band played "Hail to the Chief," the room erupted in applause for the President and First Lady. Suddenly, everyone was on their feet, applauding. This was a company town, and he was one of them. They liked that.

Even members of the opposition melded into 'One Nation of High Society' this golden evening. Sparring members of Congress warmly greeted combatant journalists with embraces. Insiders dropped their daytime faces for a good time. In doing so, they also reminded each other, beyond the public's scrutiny, that theirs was a fraternity.

That their club mattered. That many policy disagreements were little more than stagecraft. To keep the republic going, so to speak. To show diversity. Argument. And in the end, the success of comity.

The President led off with a heartfelt toast to the evening's benefactress, Mrs. Sybil Lechman. He spoke, as he often did, with tears in his eyes. He recounted his own visits with cancer patients. Of the tragedy of their worried parents. Monica couldn't stop smiling. To be here this night! With the President. To feel his genuine emotions as he reminded the audience of the reason for their attendance.

Matthew Walker always could bring matters into focus. He was taller than Monica recalled. She wondered nervously if he would remember her as the one who blabbed to the press up in New York. No sooner did she have the thought than she felt his eyes rest on her. As he spoke of health benefits, of dollars for cancer research, of his domestic program for families, his gaze was hypnotic.

David noticed the action. "Oh no, not again," he thought. He had seen Walker around beautiful women before. And Monica had insisted on wearing black, despite his warning. Well, it was her affair now. Whatever. He was about to say his good-byes anyway . . .his eyes noticed a slight movement near the dais. As he watched 'Dream Girl' go about her work at the sidelines, he recalled the day in the park. He wondered, would she remember him? *". . . fools give you reasons, wise men never try . . ."*

And so ensued for David and Monica, dual evenings devoted to romance. Just not with each other. After dinner, Monica kept edging nearer the crowd around Walker, waiting for him to notice her. To dance with her. To leave his wife for her. David chased after a certain store employee, fighting the undulating crowd that kept swallowing up the fast-moving woman with clipboard.

The party may have been in full swing, but there still were small fires to be doused. One model may have mixed drugs with her alcohol, a common occurrence among these beauties. 'Dream Girl,' of the upswept hair and floor-length designer gown, was on coffee patrol, guiding the girl to a sofa in a back office. David's search kept to the open store floors. So much more was happening behind the scenes.

One more chase of unknown consequence also was under way. The blind couple's attendant disappeared for a brief time between the main course and dessert. Alone, he made his way according to instructions to a storage area on the second floor. He found there a supply of materials that had been pre-positioned for his important task. Once he had checked everything to his professional satisfaction, he returned to the couple's side.

After dinner, 'transition music' played guests to their next activity – the live auction, taking place on the store's second floor. As super models paraded down runways flaunting high priced couturiers for the wealthy crowd, the attendant took great care to describe for his charges each fashion as it passed. As though their understanding of the exact hue of a jacket was the most important thing on the man's mind. They asked for a lot of detail. He was pleased to provide it.

As though he had all the time in the world.

As though they were his only concern.

Monica was amazed at how many people at the party knew her from her show. Many V.I.P.'s even addressed her by her character's name and asked detailed questions about coming episodes. One such individual was Senator Wes Bauers.

"Annette? From 'The Gathering Storm'? I cannot believe it is really you. Bauers is the name. Wes Bauers. 'Senator Bauers,' to most. You can call me 'Wes.'"

President Walker, bored by seeing the same people all the time, and temporarily separated from the ball and chain, searched out the beautiful blonde from dinner. When he found her, using the force of his Presidential stature and aided by a virtual wall of Secret Service agents, he easily edged out the Senator. "...*When you find your true love, when you feel her call you, across a crowded room ...*"

Their conversation transpired under the flash of news cameras. He did recall her role in the whole "Southern Prince" episode. As he spoke, he leaned in close, both for the improved view and a semblance of privacy.

"Your only mistake, my dear Miss Waters ..."

"Oh my God. He knows my name!" Monica thought.

" ... your only mistake is that you have been operating too far down the totem pole. What you really want is a seasoned man. Someone more mature than Mr. Kelly. Would I do?" he asked her.

Monica's wildest dreams were coming true. She could feel his hazel eyes peering at her in the most intimate way. It was almost as though they already were alone together, not in this crowded room. His last words were spoken over his shoulder as his overly protective Chief of Staff, Leon Barshevsky, pulled him away.

"I'll call you. We should talk."

" ... Then fly to her side and make her your own, or all through your life you may dream all alone ... "

The photos were taken. The promise was given. And twenty sets of eyes of other blonds in black dresses throughout the room angrily checked out the 'new one.' You could almost hear their collective comment.

"We don't need any outsiders in our town."

Trailing the President and his security detail at a discreet distance was the attendant to the blind couple. He stood on the periphery, just out of the agents' line of sight, and listened with mild interest to the partygoers as they approached Walker. The fawning was nearly too much to take. Walker clearly was in his element. These were his subjects. Gathered around him in his capital. Of his United States.

A woman tried to approach the attendant. She wanted to share with him how much she admired his attentiveness to his charges all evening. But the man was too quick for her. The fox sprinted behind a television camera, repositioning himself on the far side of the crowd, slightly behind a tall fichus tree.

At Walker's side, still, was Barshevsky. Leon had not yet learned of the President's pique when his face appeared next to the

Chief Executive's in too many news photos. He was not adept at deference. For this sin alone, Leon's days were numbered.

The attendant watched the two bask in the glow of television lighting. Prince and Servant. As he watched, he absent-mindedly chewed on his knuckles. Remembering his formal attire, he stopped his gnawing before he drew any blood. Now was not the time to be calling attention to himself. Instead, this was a time to practice his excellent chameleon skills. By hunching his shoulders and turning slightly to the side, he knew he could deflect people's attention from him. Later, no one would recall the rather attractive man at the party in the London custom-tailored tux.

Eventually, even Leon wore down and took a breather out of the glare of the spotlights. The attendant approached him as he stood off in a corner.

"Sir, might I have a word?"

At the question, Leon whirled around. A familiar voice. Why couldn't he place it? He looked into a pair of strangely cold, dark brown eyes. Before he could respond, he felt something sharp jab him in his side. He instinctively knew something was very wrong. Leon reacted angrily.

"Now see here. Who the devil . . ."

The toxic chemical immediately took its toll. Leon could feel his body grow numb. He tried to call out to a Secret Service agent standing nearby, but his throat already was constricting from the drug. He couldn't utter a word. Barshevsky, surrounded by a crowd, many of whom were here to guard him, was a virtual prisoner of this stranger.

Quickly, masterfully, the assassin moved Leon through the crowd to his waiting room. After the many drinks and rich food, not to mention rising decibel levels in the store, no one noticed the odd couple as they retreated to a back-storage area. The assassin latched the door and proceeded about his business.

The chemical he had administered was one known to 'the trade.' Its immediate salutary effects were to 'destabilize the subject for further trauma.' These instructions, of course, were offered in several different languages in the flyer accompanying the deadly vial. The drug's 'subject,' Leon Barshevsky was wide awake, and well aware he was in serious trouble.

The man laid Leon out on his back as he explained his plan.

"I am here to kill you, Mr. Barshevsky."

That voice. Leon struggled to focus his eyes on the man. Of course. This was his man. His own employee was doing this. Surely, there was some mistake.

"Ah yes. You know me. You have, after all, sent me on a number of dangerous missions on behalf of your president. Coming back to you now, Mr. Advisor? Yes. It is I. You killed my partner in Germany, didn't you, you son of a bitch? A man who never did anything but his best for you."

"A man who risked his life for you. Want to know how I knew it was you? The seat-belt. He always wore his seat belt. So, in part, this evening's activities are in his behalf. The lion's share, however, are in someone else's behalf. Oh, no. Do not try to speak. You can't anyway. Trust me on that one. Now then. A few words from a certain widow."

With that, the assassin pulled out a small tape player and hit the 'Play' button. Leon instantly recognized the woman's voice. He should have dealt with the bitch when he . . .

"For reasons I shall now share with you, Mr. Barshevsky, this gentleman and I would like to see you dead. Matt Walker was a decent man before he met up with the likes of you. But you saw something in him my Horace apparently missed. You found a dark and greedy side to his nature, and you have been trading on it these past several years."

"I saw your handiwork as you drove a wedge between my husband and the President. Not only have you harmed many, as attested to by my partner here, but you also have pushed the country into the hands of a damaged man. I can imagine you make of me a wealthy, flibbertigibbet of a woman, someone to be used, marginalized, and dispensed with."

"Let me advise you that, unlike yourself, I am middle America all the way. I know who I am. And I know who my Horace was. And who Matthew showed promise of being. You see, unlike yourself, I believe in the inherent goodness and morality of my country. And that is why I believe you really must go now."

"My partner and I agree on one very important thing: Revenge. And so, tonight, we shall rid the country of a bit of evil. And avenge Horace's death in the process. I'd like to tell you there will be a wing of the National Gallery of Art built in your name. But, sadly, that will not be the case."

"Good-bye Leon."

With Sybil's closing words, the assassin acted swiftly. He positioned Leon's body, cradling it in a certain way, and then waited patiently, gun in hand. Leon's terrified eyes watched the assassin's as the two sat quietly on the storeroom floor. When the fireworks sounded for the last time that evening, the man shot Leon Barshevsky. The gun was pointed down the man's throat, aimed at his brain. The sound was as one with the fireworks display, which, guests commented later, was one of the best they had ever witnessed.

"Once you have found her, never let her go."

Hours later, a security guard discovered the messy storeroom with Leon's brains scattered along the walls. By then, however, the guests had long since returned to their safe homes in the exclusive enclaves of Cleveland Park, Chevy Chase, Potomac, Georgetown.

As they slept, they knew not what tomorrow's headlines would be. Knew not the opportunities they might have on the morrow for gossip at lunch. The President's aide? Dead? Suicide, they say. Tsk, tsk. The White House is, after all, nothing but a pressure cooker. He snapped. Forensic evidence led in the direction of suicide. That, or a professional hit. Aside from a few crazy tabloid newspapers, who would ask? Who would really care?

CHAPTER FORTY-SIX

"Marley was dead, to begin with."
'A Christmas Carol,' by Charles Dickens, 1843

David woke happy. He was alone. Monica was safely ensconced across town in her luxurious hotel room. Now a friend. No longer a lover.

Thank God, David thought. To be replaced, of course, by Leslie Cameron. What had the guard called her? 'Lexi.' Suits her, he thought. It was a sunny spring day and he made coffee before finally opening the Washington Post.

The headline was writ large. The news it proclaimed, troubling. Leon Barshevsky, the President's Chief of Staff, was dead of a self-inflicted gunshot wound to the head. Found dead in a remote storage room of LeBagatelle's Department Store. The time of death was estimated to have been sometime during the previous evening's fancy gala opening.

David knew better. Suicide? 'Assassin-assisted-suicide's more like it, he thought.

As Sybil's earlier words to him replayed in his mind, David felt certain he knew the culprit's identity.

"What if a son betrays a father?"

"Where can the wife turn? Who will recompense her?"

"How severe should retribution be?"

"How close to home?"

"At what level does one take risks to avenge a death?"

No, David and Sybil had already put that subject to bed. He knew that day in Middleburg. They both agreed Horace's accident was no such thing.

And now, David felt sure, The Widow had had her day in court.

Better not to know. Too damned late for that, David thought.

As he turned to the Sunday crossword puzzle, three words replayed in his thinking:

"Six more months."

In life, as in physics, for every action, there is a reaction. In the case of Leon Barshevsky, there were in fact several reactions. The event, surrounding so prominent a figure in Washington, would be noted by many in a chronology of resolution. People needed to 'process' the information. Each, like David, reacted in their own unique way. Some had agendas to fulfill, while others simply needed to understand a hideous event.

Beginning the night before . . .

At 1:00 a.m., several models at the opening, feeling the worse for wear, failed to collect their overcoats in a storage room. 'The' storage room, as it turned out. The coats, of course, were ruined forever.

At 3:00 a.m., a cleaning crew made their way to the second floor of the store. Everything needed to be in order for the store's grand opening at noon the next day, Sunday. A janitor tried to enter a storage room to retrieve supplies, but the door seemed to be locked from the inside. He called security to unlock the room. When the two men entered the room, neither was prepared for what they saw.

The scene was unspeakably grotesque, straight from hell. A dead body was laid out in tuxedo, but its head was mostly missing . . .

blown off. Remains, blood, tissue, chunks of the man's scalp, were scattered everywhere, including the walls and ceiling. In his hands was a revolver. The men quickly left and called the police.

At 3:30 a.m., the D.C. police arrived. While murders are commonplace in the poorer neighborhoods of Washington, they rarely occur in Chevy Chase. There was the occasional domestic murder, but nothing at all like this.

Into his recorder, the D.C. captain recorded his thoughts: "White man in a tuxedo. Murdered a few feet from the President and other elected officials." And once he retrieved the man's wallet, learning the dead man's identity, he knew. Soon he was going to have a real circus on his hands.

At 4:02 a.m., "Jesus!" The Maryland 'listeners' tracking in on the captain's frequency now knew as well. Instantaneously, the news of Barshevsky's death was sent through the security system's layers up to the Central Intelligence Agency. Normally, this level of intelligence would head straight to the President via his Chief of Staff. Inconveniently, that position had been 'vacated' just twelve hours earlier.

At 5:00 a.m., the head of the C.I.A. was alerted at home. He was headed to the White House for his daily briefing. However, a cabinet meeting this day was to precede his briefing. Word had it that some cabinet heads would roll today. He knew Walker's temper. While the American people had elected a steady hand at the helm, they had gotten the opposite. The worse matters became, the more tightly wound was Matt Walker.

What man in his right mind would call the President just two hours before a political blood bath to tell him his trusted aide was dead? After considerable reflection, the C.I.A. man decided the messenger in this situation had a better than even chance of being shot. Or, more likely, seeing his own name added to the list of those being shown the door.

The man could just hear his angry president now: "How could the nation's intelligence service let this happen? Under your very noses?"

So, the intelligence man made an executive decision. One any fellow cabinet member, under the circumstances, would readily understand.

Stand down.

Wait for the light of day.

Deal with it later.

At 6:00 p.m., the forensics team completed its investigation.
Early inside word had it as a professional hit. That, or a suicide. Take
your pick. What were they, stupid? The initial paperwork ruled the
cause of death as a self-inflicted gunshot wound to the head. The guys
on site, however, homicide professionals, the best in the business, had
to admire the assassin's work. Whoever did this, they had to hand it to
the guy. He definitely knew his stuff.

By 7:00 a.m., the word was out about Leon's death. Even the
White House press corps, often the last to know, knew. Nearly
everyone in town, by now, knew. Except for one man. That man was
busy preparing for his meeting. He had not read the morning papers.
The wife had slept in that day. No aide dared approach. And so,
Matthew Walker strode confidently into his cabinet meeting, ready to
announce a few staff changes.

In the room, the air was quiet with tension. Walker glanced
around the room and barked, "Where's Leon?"

The President's question was met by stunned silence. How
could he not know? Finally, his Agriculture Secretary stepped up. And
told the last person in Washington the sad news.

By 10:00 a.m., all the major news media had their story. The death was a confirmed suicide. Later in the week, a TV talk show featured psychiatrists discussing the topic 'Suicide. It Could Happen to You.' While most media took the suicide pill without blinking, the tabs' headlines, true to form, screamed 'Who Killed Leon Barshevsky?' The President met with Leon's widow.

And made calm arrangements for his replacement.

As the President re-staffed and the Barshevsky family grieved, Sybil rejoiced. A dead man's body stashed in Le Bagatelle's storage room was just fine with her, so long as it was Leon's. Even better, it should be Matthew's, with his head blown off. But even Sybil knew when to stop.

The only surprise in the whole adventure for her was her total lack of regret. That said, she did follow the news reports with morbid fascination. Watched the back-to- back cable coverage of suicide, 'the disease.' Listened to talk show guests discuss depression. Heard talking heads opine about the difficulty of working at the White House, the world's most difficult workplace.

She even laughed out loud during one show when an author announced his new book, 'Ten Steps to Not Committing Suicide.'

"If only he knew," she thought bitterly. "'Step One' – Do not order my husband's death."

CHAPTER FORTY-SEVEN

"When you come to a fork in the road, take it."
Yogi Berra

David's sons were served lunch onboard United's Flight 173 from Seattle to Virginia's Dulles International Airport. Snorkel gear stuck out of their kit bags as they flew to meet their father for Spring Break. The three men were soon leaving for a St. John's Island camping trip.

Josh and Kenny Kelly were excited about the plane trip and the island part. But most of all, they missed their dad. They liked the way he listened to them when they told him their stories.

Two brothers about the same age as David's sons also were embarking on an exciting adventure. Their father had just purchased a new five-million-dollar motor sailor on which their family was soon to set sail across the ocean. The boys had their own bedroom aft, their parents a luxury suite forward, near the bulkhead. They carefully helped their father load the boat as it floated at anchor in Annapolis Harbor.

Later, as the attractive family boarded the beautiful teak craft for their departure, others watched them with envy. In Annapolis, one can tell 'blue water' boats by the level of sophisticated navigational equipment they carry. This beauty obviously was bound for the world.

People at the dock watched the man weigh anchor and start the boat's substantial engines. Father and sons wore matching navy wool sweaters. The man grabbed ahold of the wheel with masterful, neatly manicured hands, and the boat backed from its slip. What a sight they all were. Once the sleek craft reached the Bay's shipping lane, it gradually faded from view.

An hour after President Walker's infamous cabinet meeting, the White House issued a statement announcing the cabinet changes. Layton got the word third-hand. He was out. That meant David also was out. Both men saw it coming, and with the news, David felt lighter and happier than he had felt in a long, long time.

There was the requisite news conference at the Department of Resource Development. Attendance was slim – most of the reporters remained camped out at the White House awaiting further bulletins on the Leon matter. One reporter asked the Secretary if his leaving had anything to do with calling the President a 'Southern Prince.' Both Layton and Kelly laughed at the question. Which was, of course, the point. Now, they could laugh. It was again permitted. Damaged people

346

don't laugh. Healthy people do. And both men already were now on the road to recovery.

Later, Layton's secretary, Marge, asked David to lunch. They went to a small restaurant in Georgetown, a family place frequented by Hunt Country regulars. The tavern-restaurant was dark with private leather booths. Seated beneath the horsey lithographs, David recalled seeing David Eisenhower lunching with Bob Woodward. Because of both men's attendance at the same Navy prep school, he always wondered if Eisenhower might have been one of Woodward's Watergate sources.

They took a back booth. There was a lot to discuss. Better it be done in privacy. Kelly began the conversation with an air of normality.

"We've been together six years now. Are you planning to stay on -- work for Layton's replacement?"

"I know what you did."

David sat up straight. "Marge, I don't know . . ."

"You went through my desk. You read my papers. You broke locks like a common thief."

" .. . I'd like to think, I was uncommon." Kelly tried for lightness. His remark fell with a thud.

"What do you think you know, Kelly?"

"Well, plenty. I know that Layton and Walker have been on the outs for some time now. At least since before our trip to Japan. I know these trips of Layton's to Japan weren't on the up and up . . ."

"You don't know anything."

The two sat in silence as their drinks were delivered. It was a stand-off. David had no way of knowing where the conversation would head next. He had his hopes. He wanted some closure here. Marge began again.

"I have been damaged. Compromised. Probably broken all sorts of laws. My loyalty to the Secretary has been stretched to the breaking point. Thank God it's over. You had no right . . ."

David interrupted. "Now hold on. You just said I know nothing. Now, you're bringing me into it."

"You are on the Walker team."

"For that matter, so are you."

"Not in the same way. You know that. Anyway, it doesn't matter anymore. You worked on the Wilderness Bill. I think you need to own that."

David had no idea. "Hell, yes, I'll 'own it.' It's a good bill. Saving the wilderness. For our kids to enjoy."

"You honestly believe that crap?"

"Marge, listen. It's not crap."

"Crap. It's land that's being saved alright. But for what? For whom?"

This much closure David could have done without. Couldn't he just leave town now, quietly, with years served? Apparently not. Apparently, he was going to know, the bird on the ledge, whether or not he wanted.

"Oh my God. Then it is true."

"What?"

"I saw this article in the back of Layton's car not long ago. About some deformed animals out in Wyoming."

"Getting warmer. Let me just tell you. This makes me want to throw up. The trips to Japan? The money? Put the two together, Kelly. For God's sake!"

"Japan was paying to use the land for . . ."

Then, Marge confirmed it. He already knew. But now he really knew. For good and all.

" . . the dumping of nuclear waste."

David recalled the UniStar note to the President. He didn't mention it. Instead, he said, "But Marge, everyone knows Japan is not a member of the nuclear family."

"Is too."

"Is not."

"Is too. But hardly anyone knows it. You, for instance. I know you saw that UniStar note. Stop playing dumb with me, Kelly."

David gave up. He brought the rest of himself along to the lunch.

"Let me ask you this. Is there any evidence tying Walker to the payments?"

"Kelly, what do you need, an affidavit? Alright, alright. There was a note once. From Leon Barshevsky . . . something about there being a limit to the amount that could be stored in this one park. I did not say any of this. Layton . . ."

Marge dropped her voice down low.

" . . Layton sort of . . . shared the note with someone. A person who can put a stop to this shit. The guys . . . you know, the big guys . . . now know what Walker's been up to."

David let out a breath of amazement.

"So . . ."

Marge finished the conversation: " . . . so, you're off the hook. So's Layton. The Wilderness Legislation is real again. And the shenanigans should be over soon. Kelly, you clear town. Just remember, it was never Layton. It was never him. He is a wonderful, honorable man. And so are you. End of story. Now, kindly buy me another drink."

The two had several more drinks, barely touching their lunch. The restaurant was known for its fresh produce. Neither of them noticed. If it was closure David needed, it was contained in this talk. In what Marge had said. They had each played their roles. Some knew more than others.

No one, it seemed, besides Leon and the President knew the entire story. No one except the secretary. Always the secretary. They see the papers. The traffic. Take the calls. Can add and subtract. Surmise and conclude. That was Marge. She had told David the score and left him with renewed trust in Jeffrey Layton. They had been duped. The age of innocence was now over. For them all.

There had developed in the last few years a group of party elders who had splintered off from Matthew Walker. If push came to shove, they still would hew to the party line. But they were beginning to think for themselves again. Slowly but surely, they were rebuilding the party from the inside out again. On principles of sound conduct and high-minded goals.

Layton was finished with politics, mostly due to his age. But he knew David still had some good years left in him. He also recognized in his boy the fires of moral indignation just beneath the surface. In deference to those fires, and as promised, Layton saw to some arrangements. There were some excellent political candidates out west who could benefit from David's fine hand. Layton matched them up. The Secretary had many things on his conscience as he left office. David Kelly, he resolved, would not be one.

The rain began in the nation's capital. At first, it was a fine mist. Then it became a steady torrent, as unrelenting as a death sentence. Tucked into his Foggy Bottom place, with fires going in both fireplaces, and his two sons in residence, David thought it could rain all it wanted. No amount of inclement weather could wipe the smile off his face today.

David was glad they weren't leaving for the island for another day. Perhaps the sun would come out in time for their departure. He fixed his sweet sons their favorite French toast for breakfast. After they chose a movie to see later, he proposed a little time outside in the rain.

So, off they ran, three Northwestern males, undaunted by a little moisture. They entered the path to Rock Creek Park. David knew an open area where he could run and the boys would have room to kick around their soccer ball. Once they were happily playing, David took a lap circling them. His hair was dripping wet, but he didn't care, he was so damned happy. He had a new job. His boys. What more could he ask?

Just then, around the corner came another runner. A woman. A woman who had been outside long enough that her shoes sloshed with every step. A woman with a long reddish braid hanging down her back. 'Dream Girl.'

This time, David took no chances. He stepped directly in her path, holding out his arms to catch her. Startled, 'Dream Girl' looked up into a pair of intelligent, laughing hazel eyes. David looked familiar to her in a comfortable sort of way, almost as though she knew him. The two stood there, as the rain came down, laughing over nothing.

Finally, recalling their manners, they exchanged names.

David began. "I know who you are. You were at that party at Le Bagatelle's, the one last week."

Their conversation continued. Two crazy people standing in a driving rainstorm discussing their jobs . . . running . . . their lives. Eventually, 'Dream Girl,' mentioned her accident. And held up a newly-healed foot for David to see.

He was sympathetic.

"Washington can be a dangerous town. You never can tell when someone's going to knock you over."

EPILOGUE

"Look at every path closely and deliberately. Try it as many times as you think necessary. Then ask yourself, and yourself alone, one question. This question is one that only a very old man asks. My benefactor told me about it once when I was young, and my blood was too vigorous for me to understand it. Now I do understand it. I will tell you what it is: Does this path have a heart? All paths are the same: they lead nowhere. They are paths going through the bush, or into the bush. In my own life I could say I have traversed long, long paths, but I am not anywhere. My benefactor's question has meaning now. Does this path have heart? If it does, the path is good; if it doesn't, it is of no use. Both paths lead nowhere; but one has a heart, the other doesn't. One makes for a joyful journey; as long as you follow it, you are one with it. The other will make you curse your life. One makes you strong; the other weakens you."
Don Juan, Quoted in 'The Teachings of Don Juan,' by Carlos Castaneda

---

Secretary Layton

Was divorced. He and Sybil eventually were married and retired to the Montego Bay home.

Leon Barshevsky's

Funeral was attended only by his immediate family. The President sent his regrets.

357

Monica
Was offered a role in a major motion picture, the result of her Washington notoriety.

The Assassin, Frank, to his friends
Retired from 'the business,' and moved his family to a small farm in Patagonia,

President Walker,
With one of the largest campaign war chests in history, was overwhelmingly reelected. His legacy as The Wilderness President, however, was denied him by a few men who knew the truth.

David and 'Dream Girl'
Fell in love. Together, they returned to snow-capped mountains, the Pacific Ocean, and David's two sons. They were married last Tuesday.

FADEOUT

BASED ON THE AWARD-WINNING PLAY, "SAY UNCLE!" AND WARNER BROTHERS DRAFT SCREENPLAY.

Karen Hagestad Cacy is also the author of the following novels:

R.S.V.P.
The Reluctant Spy
Murder at Pebble Beach

Her other credits include:

SAY UNCLE! a two-act play
SAY UNCLE! a screenplay

A graduate of Portland State University, she also attended American University in Cairo and George Washington University. A former cabinet-level speechwriter and federal transportation lobbyist, she now lives in Colorado Springs, Colorado, where she is at work on her fifth novel.

Contact: cacywrites@gmail.com
Website: www.cacywrites.com